Ariel
Percy Bysshe Shelley

Poetry and History for the world citizens of today and tomorrow.

Ariel Percy Bysshe Shelley
Illustrated Unabridged New Edition

First published in paperback special edition, 2025
By Cybirdy Publishing
101 Camley Street, London N1C 4DU, UK

This book is sold subject to the condition that it shall not,
By way of trade, digitalisation or otherwise, be lent, resold, hired
Out or otherwise circulated without the publisher's prior consent
In any form of binding or cover other than that in which it is
Published and without a similar condition being imposed
On the subsequent purchaser.

Original work first written in French by André Maurois in 1923

Translated by Alix Daniel
Cover page and Illustrations by Anwot
Printed by Hobbs the Printer, UK

This book is typeset in minion, Proxima Nova and Copperplate.
A CIP record for this book is available from the British Library

ISBN: 978-1-0686782-6-4

ARIEL
PERCY BYSSHE SHELLEY
NEW TRANSLATION

ANDRÉ MAUROIS
TRANSLATED BY ALIX DANIEL

CYBIRDY
Publishing Limited

PART ONE

So I turned to the Garden of Love
That so many sweet flowers bore;
And I saw it was filled with graves.

William Blake

1
DR KEATE'S METHOD

In 1809, King George III appointed Doctor John Keate as Eton College's headmaster. He was a small and terrible man, who considered beating as a necessary method to lead to moral perfection. Doctor Keate used to end his sermons saying: "Be charitable, my boys, otherwise I shall beat you until you so become."

The gentlemen and wealthy merchants whose sons were educated by him were not appalled at all by this pious ferocity and actually considered highly the man who was known to have whipped most of the ministers, bishops and generals in the country.

Indeed, it was a time when any strict discipline was approved by the elite. The recent French Revolution had been a demonstration of the dangers of liberalism, specifically when it spreads among the country's leaders. Officially, England, the soul of the Holy Alliance, believed that fighting against Napoleon meant fighting against the French philosophy. So, it asked its public schools for a generation of obedient hypocrites.

With the purpose of taming the possible zeal of the young aristocrats, their studies were deliberately superficial.

After five years of studies, the student had read Homer twice, nearly completed Virgil, expurgated Horace and was able to compose Latin epigrams of average quality about Wellington or even Nelson. The taste for quotes was so much perfected among them that once, when Pitt stopped in the middle of a verse from the *Aeneid*, the whole Parliament chamber, Whigs and Tories alike, arose and finished off the verse. A perfect example of a homogeneous culture!

Science was optional and so neglected; dance was compulsory. As for religion, Keate deemed any doubt about it as a crime. Talking about religion was useless. In fact, the doctor feared mysticism more than indifference. He tolerated laughter in church and was indifferent about the Sabbath. It is important to point out here the Machiavellianism of this educator. He would tolerate a few little lies. "A sign of respect," he used to say.

Somewhat barbaric customs were at the centre of student life. The little ones (youngest) were referred to as the fags, or the slaves of the big ones (elders). Each fag had to make the bed of his master, pump up water for him or even brush his clothes and shoes. Any disobedience was sanctioned by appropriate torments. One child wrote to his parents, not to complain, but just to describe his day at school: "My master, wanted me to jump over a too large ditch, just like a horse. Each time I shirked, he spurred me. As the result my thigh is bleeding, my Greek poets' small book is reduced to a pulp and my brand-new clothes are torn apart."

Boxing was an honourable sport. One day, a fight got so violent that one child was killed in the ring. Keate came to see the dead body and said: "This is a shame. However, I demand that each student from Eton to be ready to trade tit for tat in any circumstances."

The ultimate but hidden objective of the system was to build strong characters from one unique mould. Autonomy of action was important. However, showing creativity in thinking or clothing, or even in the use of language, was the most despised crime. Even the slightest fervour for study or ideas was considered an intolerable tendency which required beating.

As it was, this life was far from displeasing for the young British elite. The pride they derived from being part of the continuing tradition of such an old school, created by the king and forever close to and protected by royalty, was worth the suffering.

A few souls suffered, though, and for a long time. For example, the young Percy Bysshe Shelley, son of a rich landowner in Sussex and grandson of Sir Bysshe Shelley, baronet. He did not seem to fit in with this education. The child, extremely beautiful, with clear blue and sharp eyes, curled blond hair, and a delicate constitution, demonstrated moral scruples quite unusual for a man of his rank, together with an unusual tendency to question the rules.

At the time of his arrival at school, the sixth form's captains, seeing his frail body, girlish gestures and angelic face, imagined a shy character who would not challenge their authority too much.

However, they soon found out that Shelley was quick to react to any danger with passion. An unwavering will, in a body too weak to physically resist, made him prone to rebellion. His eyes had the kindness of a dreamer when at rest. However, enthusiasm or outrage gave them a nearly wild sparkle, while his voice, usually serious and sweet, became shrill and soared.

His love of books and disdain for games, his hair flying in the wind and his shirt open to a feminine neck, everything shocked the censors in charge of maintaining the elegant brutality the school was proud of.

Having decided, from his first day at Eton, that the tyranny against the fags was against human dignity, Shelley refused point blank to serve. This made him considered disloyal.

He was called 'Shelley the mad boy'. The most powerful of the tormentors opted for his salvation by torture, but avoided attacking him in single combat, thinking he was able of anything. He fought like a girl, with open hands, slapping and scratching.

DR KEATE'S METHOD

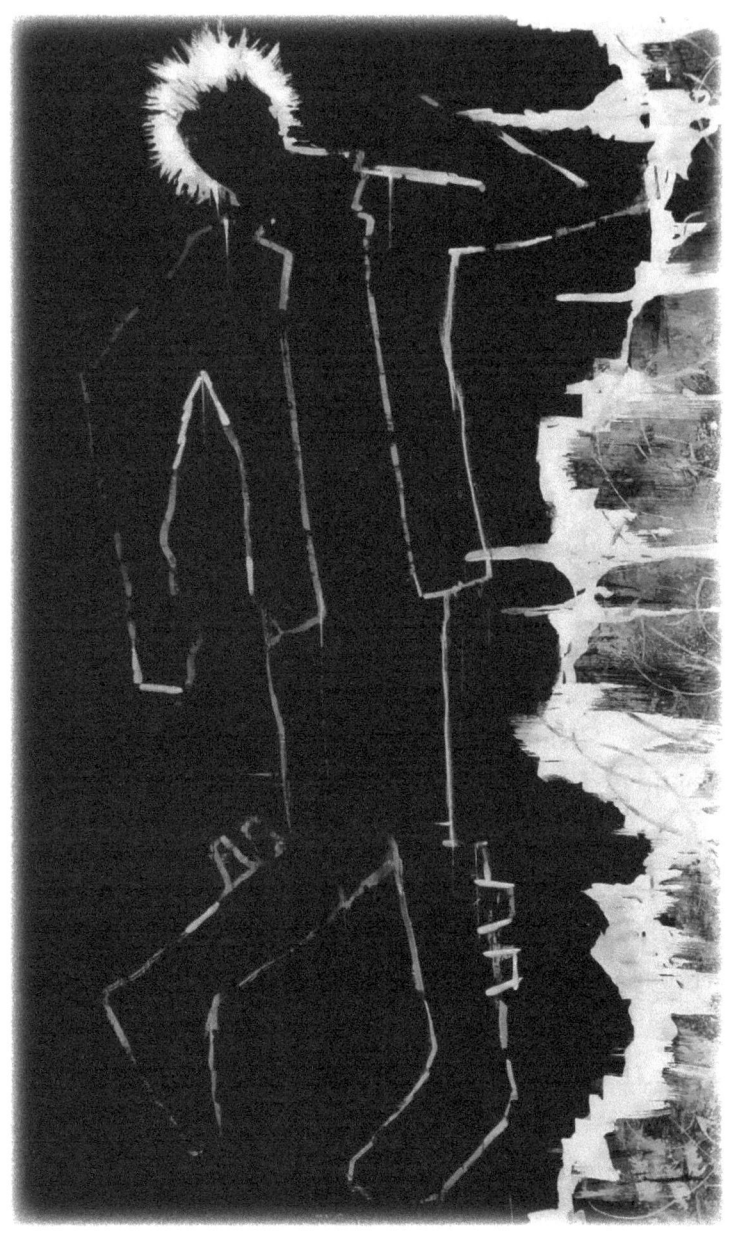

In an organised pack, the hunt for Shelley became one of the big games at Eton. When hunters found the odd being reading a poem on the riverbank, they immediately alerted the others. Hair flying in the wind, Shelley tried to flee, across the meadows, to the street of the town or the college's cloister. Finally, stopped and surrounded against a wall, squeezed like a wild boar at bay, he uttered a piercing shrill scream. Then, in the mud, the mob of students fired words and nailed him to the wall. One voice shouted: "Shelley!" "Shelley!" answered another voice. The old grey walls echoed the scream "Shelley!" in shrill tones. A sycophant fag held the tortured victim's clothes, another one pinched him while a third quietly approached and kicked with his boots Shelley's book, which he was trying to hold desperately against his arm.

And then, all fingers pointed at the victim, and a new scream: "Shelley! Shelley! Shelley!" was the last straw. Finally, the crisis, anticipated by the bullies, happened. A fit of insane fury made his eyes sparkle, his cheeks turned pale and his limbs shook.

Then, tired of the now monotonous show, the whole school went back to its games. Shelley picked up his mud-stained book. All alone and deep in his thoughts, slowly he walked towards the beautiful meadows of the Thame's bank. Sitting on the sun-dappled grass, he stayed and watched the river gliding by.

Running water has, just like music, the gentle power to transform sadness in melancholia. Both, music and running water slowly seep into the soul the certainty of oblivion, because of their inevitable and continuous natural flow. The massive towers of Windsor and of Eton erected around the rebel child an immutable and hostile universe, but the trembling willow tree calmed him by its own fragility.

He was always going back to his books. It was Diderot, Voltaire and the system of nature by Holbach. He felt courageous in admiring these French writers scorned by Eton's masters. One title summarised his being: *An Enquiry Concerning Political Justice* by Godwin. So much so that it became his favourite reading. Godwin's theory made everything appear so simple and logical.

If every human being was reading it, people would live in an idyllic world. If they would listen to the voice of reason, that is, Godwin's voice, two hours of work a day would be sufficient to nourish them all. Free love would replace the complications of marriage. Philosophy would replace superstitious fears. Sadly, preconceptions and prejudice were there to stay and to harden the hearts.

Shelley closed his book, lay down in the sun, and, surrounded by flowers, he meditated about human misery. From the medieval buildings of the nearby school, a limited murmur of stupidity drifted to these charming woods and brooks. Around him, in the quiet countryside, no mocking face was looking at him, though. At last, the child allowed his tears to flow, and, holding his hands tightly together, he pronounced this strange oath: " I swear to be good, fair and free, as much as I can; I swear to never be an accomplice, even with my silence, of the selfish and powerful people. I swear to dedicate my life to Beauty…"

If Dr Keate had witnessed this fit of religious fervour, so reprehensible in such a well-maintained English institution, he would certainly have addressed the case with his favourite method.

2
HOME

On holidays, the refractory slave became the crown prince. His father, Mr Timothy Shelley, owned the manor of Field-Place in Sussex. It was a long white house, well built, surrounded by a park and large woods. Shelley found there his four sisters, all pretty, his young brother aged 3, whom he already taught to shout "Devil"! to scandalise bigots, and his beautiful cousin, Harriet, who looked exactly like him.

The head and ancestor of the family, Sir Bysshe Shelley, lived in the village. He was a gentleman from the English old school, who liked to say he was as rich as a duke but lived like a poacher. Six feet tall, impressive with a beautiful face, his wit was both sharp and cynical. It was from him that the Shelley family inherited their blue and flashing eyes.

He spent £80,000 building a castle he never lived in, due to the necessary upkeep costs. Rather, he was living in a small cottage with only one servant. Most of the day he stayed at the local pub, dressed like a farmer, and talked politics to travellers. From America, he brought back a kind of brutal humour which shocked the easy-going English people. Two of his daughters were so unhappy with him that one day they flew: excellent alibi for not giving them any dowry. His only desire was to build wealth, which was already immense, to transmit to countless generations of Shelleys to come. To that objective, he placed the largest part to Percy, who would inherit, excluding his brothers and sisters. Considering his grandson as the continuation of his posthumous ambition, he had a certain fondness for him. As for his son, Timothy, the one who pontificated, he simply despised him.

Mr Timothy Shelley, a Member of Parliament, was like his father, tall and handsome, blond and impressive. He had more heart than Bysshe; however, his will was not as sharp. Sir Bysshe, a selfish lord, was nonetheless attractive with his natural charm of the cynic. On the contrary, Mr Timothy had good intentions which made him insufferable. He used to love words with the irritating clumsiness of the illiterate. He demonstrated a worldly respect for religion, and an aggressive tolerance for new ideas together with a pompous philosophy. He liked to refer to himself as a liberal in his political and religious opinions. However, he avoided shocking the people around him. As a close friend of the Catholic Duke of Norfolk, he talked complacently about Irish Catholic emancipation, a great audacity he was proud, yet scared of. Occasionally, he wept but could become ferocious if his self-esteem was at risk. In his private life, he was tempted to reconcile gentle gestures with despotic actions. Diplomatic about trivial things, he was harsh about important ones. Harmless yet irritating, he was made to annoy any critic.

It is indubitable that the annoyance caused by his father's talkative stupidity largely contributed to throw Shelley into an intellectual wilderness.

As for Mrs Shelley, she had been the prettiest young girl in Sussex once. She appreciated a man who was a fighter and a horseman and watched with irony her elder son walking to the forest with a book under his arm rather than a gun.

In his sisters' eyes, Shelley was superhuman. As soon as he was back from Eton, the house was inhabited by fantastic guests. Mr Timothy's Park became animated with a babble of murmurs, such as *A Midsummer Night's Dream,* and the young girls experienced fearful excitement.

He took pleasure in infusing mystery within quiet objects of everyday life. In holes of the old walls, he used to sink a stick to look for any possible secret path. In the attic, he discovered a bedroom that was always locked up. There, he said, lived an old alchemist with a long beard, the terrible Cornelius Agrippa. When one heard some noise coming from the attic, it was thought to be Cornelius knocking over his lamp. And then, for one whole week, the Shelley family worked in the garden to dig a summer haven for Cornelius.

At the arrival of the student, other monsters awoke. There was the big turtle that lived in the pond, and an old snake, a scary reptile who once upon a time had really lived in the thickets of the park but got killed by one of Mr Timothy's gardeners' scythe. "This gardener, little girls, this gardener who looked like a normal human being like you and I, is in reality Time itself, which makes legendary monsters all perish."

What was making these inventions so charming was the fact that the teller was unsure if he was creating them from scratch or not. Stories of witches and ghosts had troubled his own sensitive childhood. However, the more Shelley feared the apparitions, the more he made himself confront them. As an example, he took on the habit of drawing a circle on the ground, then in the circle, set alight a saucer filled with alcohol, and then, gazing at the bluish flame, he started an incantation: "Demons of the air and fire… There!"

"What are you doing, Shelley?" his master at Eton once asked. It was the pompous and magnificent Bethell who interrupted him on this occasion. To which Shelley replied, "Please, sir, I evoke the Devil."

In the countryside too, the lord of darkness was called upon with a high-pitched but firm young voice. On occasion, the children, full of joy, welcomed their sovereign brother's order to dress up as spirits and devils. In reality, chemistry explained the mysterious alchemy in these romantic games. Scientific discipline was foreign to Shelley, he preferred the magical aspects of science. On one occasion, armed with a machine he had just created, he gave electric shocks to the respectful battalion of young girls. When the youngest one, little Helen, saw him armed with a bottle and a metal thread, she started to cry.

He had two trusty and loving disciples: the oldest of his sisters, Elisabeth, and his cousin in law, Harriet Grove. A nascent sensuality, together with a passionate search for truth, united the three. The first stirrings of desire always communicate to the mind the natural and powerful charm of caresses.

One day, Shelley guided his beautiful students towards the cemetery, a special location where the mysterious presence of the dead appeared to him as poetical. Sitting down on a rustic tomb, protected from Mr Timothy's eyes by the shadow of the old church, he embraced their flexible waists, and then talked about the world and its gods, addressing the beautiful and attentive four eyes.

He drew a simple picture of the universe. On one side, vice: kings, priests and rich people; on the other side, virtue: philosophers and the poor. On one side, religion at the service of tyranny; on the other side, Godwin's *Enquiry Concerning Political Justice*.

But most of all, he talked to them about love.

Law makers claim to impose rules on our natural feelings. What insanity! When the eye spots a charming being, the heart ignites. How can one prevent this? On the other hand, love can only wither if constrained, because its essence is freedom itself. Love is incompatible with obedience, jealousy or fear. It needs trust and abandonment. Marriage is a jail…

However, the reality is that scepticism about marriage does not appeal to young, unmarried women. Metaphysical sacrilege seldom amuses them; matrimonial sacrilege smells like faggots to their charming noses.

"Relationship?" Harriet used to say. "Maybe… but whatever, if those relationships are gentle?"

"If they are gentle, they are useless. Does one shackle a voluntary prisoner?"

"…but religion…"

Shelley called Holbach in aid of Godwin.

"If God is fair, how can one believe that he punishes creatures he has himself filled with weaknesses? If he is all mighty, how can one offend him, how can one resist? If he is reasonable, how could he get upset with the unfortunates he gave the freedom to be unreasonable?"

"The customs…"

"Should these customs, from a short period of eternity, which we refer as the 19th century, bother us, really?"

Elisabeth was a supporter of her brother. As for Harriet, could she debate with a half god with sparkling eyes, his shirt half open on a delicate neck and with fine hair resembling golden silk threads?

"Let's work on *Zastrozzi*, shall we?" she whispered, in an attempt to change the subject.

It was a novel on which all three were working. There was the thief who was the righter of wrongs, the haughty and cynical tyrant and the heroine who was elegant and proportionate, wholly kind and pure. Writing *Zastrozzi* meant hours gently passed by. Soon, the night was taking them by surprise. Elisabeth, sister and complicit, left in the shadows the two ingenuous lovers.

Shelley and Harriet came back, hugging each other in the white mist coming up from the meadows. In the small forest protecting them from sight, a light wind swayed the highest branches across the face of the moon. The anemones, closing their corollas, curved their tired stems; the melancholia of the site reminded Shelley about his imminent arrival back at Eton's dark cloisters. However, feeling the trembling and vibrations of his cousin's warm body beneath his hand, he felt courageous and full of strength to face a life ahead of battles for his calling.

3
THE COMPANION

In October 1810, Mr Timothy brought his son up to Oxford University. The Member of Parliament was in good spirits. He stayed at an old inn, signposted the 'Leaden Horse'. He met there Mr Slatter who was the son of Mr Shelley's former landlord, whom he had succeeded in the lodging-house and plumbing business. He announced that he came to register the future baronet in the very college where he himself sparkled once, for a short time. Such ceremonies are always welcome to an English gentleman. He went to the library and Mr Slatter opened for his son an account with an unlimited allowance for books and paper. "My son here," Mr Timothy said, pointing out with good heartedness the young man with crazy hair and sparkling eyes, "Mr Slatter, my son is a literary man. As a matter of fact, he is already the author of a novel, the famous *Zastrozzi*. In the event he desires to be published again, I expect you to let him achieve this caprice."

Shelley was delighted with life at the college. To have a room of one's own, to be free to attend or not the lectures, to be able to work on subjects of one own's choice, to read, write, to wander as one wished: All of this merged the joys of life in a monastery with the freedom of a philosopher's spirit. It was how he wished to live the rest of his life.

That evening, in the large hall, he was sitting close to a young man, a newcomer just like him, who, after he had named himself as Jefferson Hogg, observed great discretion, as was the tradition in Oxford. However, in the middle of the meal, incapable of keeping the elegant silence anymore, the two young men started to talk about their respective reading.

"The best literature of today is German," said Shelley. Hogg, with a smile on his face replied and argued that German literature was not quite natural, though. He felt tired of so much unrealistic romanticism.

"Which modern literature would you compare it with?"

"Italian," he said.

This conversation awoke Shelley's foolhardiness, and a boundless speech gushed out of his mouth. It became impossible for the servants to clear the tables before the two young gentlemen realised that they were left all alone.

"Would you like to come up to my room?" said Hogg. "We shall continue with our discussion."

Shelley eagerly agreed. However, while going upstairs, he lost the conversation's thread together with any interest in German literature. While Hogg lit the candles, his guest said quietly that he did not see how this discussion could carry on, since he did not know anything about Italian let alone German literature and that he actually talked only for the purpose of it.

While setting the table with a bottle, two glasses and some biscuits, Hogg smiled and replied that his detachment and his ignorance were about the same.

"Besides," said Shelley, "literature is without real significance. What does it mean to study an ancient language or even a modern one? Learning new words to name things; would it not be wiser to learn about these very things?"

"These very things?" said Hogg. "But how?"

"With chemistry, for example."

Being more inspired by it than German literature, Shelley started a lecture about chemical analysis and new discoveries in physics and electricity.

Hogg, who was not particularly interested in these subjects, closely inspected his new friend. He was perfectly dressed, with special care, but his clothes were disordered; slim, fragile, very tall, Shelley sometimes seemed stooped. In the fire of his enthusiasm, he tended to elongate his head straight forward. His gestures were both graceful and violent, he had messy long hair, and, just like a woman, his face was pale and of a pink tone. The whole face was breathing fire with a permanent animation and a wit all together supernatural. Furthermore, the expression of his morality was no less impressive than his mind, he could feel an air of kindness, gentleness and of religious fervour which reminded him the heads of saints to be seen in Florence frescoes.

Shelley was still talking when the clock struck. He shouted, "My mineralogy lesson!" and then disappeared into the corridor.

* * *

Hogg had made a promise to come to him the next morning. He found Shelley in an agitated discussion with the cleaner who wanted to clean his room.

Books, shoes, papers, pistols, clothes, munitions, flasks and test tubes were all over the floor. An electrical machine, an air pump, and a solar microscope towered above the chaos. Shelley turned the crank handle of the machine. Suddenly, from all sides, dry sparks crackled. He climbed on a stool made of glass and his long hair all stood up. Hogg, bemused, followed his movements with some concern, and looked out for the tea plates and dishes. His guest was about to serve tea, when Shelley hastily removed a penny that was at the bottom of the cup, gnawed by chloric acid.

The two young men became inseparable. Every morning, they would go together for a walk. Shelley behaved like a child, running to the top of the bank and jumping over the ditches. When they reached a pond or a river, he used to launch boats made of paper and followed them till shipwrecked. Meanwhile, Hogg, infuriated, waited on the bank.

After the walk, they used to go upstairs to Shelley's room, where Shelley, exhausted by his hyperactivity, fell into an immediate torpor. He lay down opposite the fireplace, huddled like a cat and slept as such from 6 to 10 in the morning. And then, suddenly, he would wake up and stand up while violently rubbing his eyes and then passing his fingers through his hair. On the spot, he would start talking about a precise metaphysical issue or recite verses with a nearly painful energy.

At 11, he would eat. His meals were not complicated at all. Hostile in principle to meat, he just loved bread. He always had some in his pockets, and when he was walking, he used to nibble some while reading, such that his path was often marked by a long trail of crumbs. Along with bread, his favourite food was raisins and dry damson plums that one could buy at the grocer's. He found meals sitting at the table excruciating and boring. It was unusual if he stayed sitting until the end of the meal.

After eating, his mind was clear and inquisitive, and his speech just brilliant. He talked to Hogg about his cousin Harriet, to whom he used to write lengthy letters, where surges of love alternated with Godwin's philosophy; about his sister Elisabeth, so valiantly opposed to prejudice. Or else he used to read Mr Timothy's most recent pompous letter with bursts of laughter. Then, he used to grasp one of his favourite books, by Locke, Hume or Voltaire to comment it with passion.

Hogg always wondered why the sceptics were attractive for his friend's mind, which was so obviously mystical and religious. It seems that in discovering through his reading the infinite variety of systems that could be compared to an entanglement of deep valleys and rocky precipices, a kind of dizziness overcame Shelley and that only one clear and simple theory, like the one developed by Godwin, could calm down this metaphysical drunkenness.

It was like he was taking delight in replacing the huge and confusing heap made by history with a see-through structure made of empty and clear theorems. It seems he ended up preferring a clear theory than the real world. Its incoherence frightened him because he used to visualise multitude of things through ethereal fortifications of his mind.

When the college clock struck 2 in the afternoon, Hogg woke up, and, despite his friend's complaints, simply left: "What a surprising being, he thought while crossing the long silent corridor to reach his room… the grace of a young woman, the purity of a virgin who has never left her mother's wing, and yet, an incorruptible power, a soul of a Benedictine monk with the ideas of a revolutionary."

Shelley's words were, as a matter of fact, a reasonable mixture of reflections. However, Master Jefferson Hogg did not like the tiresome meditations, and his friend Shelley quite often inspired in him the desire to sleep.

4
THE NEARBY PINE TREE

A few days before Christmas, Mr Timothy found in his mail a letter from a London publisher with the name of Mr Stockdale. It was about some unusual writing that Percy Shelley had asked him to print.

Mr Stockdale had in fact been given the manuscript of a novel full of the most subversive ideas: *St Irvyne, or the Rosicrucian: A Romance*. Mr Stockdale, a righteous businessman, was quite concerned that the son of a respectable man was taking such a perilous path. He found it necessary and his duty to both alert the father and to speak out against the young Shelley's fallen angel, Jefferson Hogg, the son of a Tory, from a good family from the north of England, but with a wicked mind, twisted and dangerous.

Mr Timothy informed Mr Stockdale that he would not pay anything towards any of the printing. However, his reply instantly aggravated the metaphysical and ideological worries of the publisher.

Thereafter, while awaiting his son's arrival at Field-Place for the Christmas holidays, Mr Timothy prepared what he would say to him. Passionate and incoherent, like a scary admonition, it was full of solemnity and stupidity, the literary genre of which he was a master.

Reasoning never convinces anyone. Besides, trusting you can reason your own son to make him change his ideas is reaching the height of lunacy.

Shelley left this conversation upset by his family's stupidity but also furious about the behaviour of Mr Stockdale. It was unworthy of a gentleman. Furthermore, he felt closer to his friend, Jefferson Hogg. The same night, he wrote him a long letter in confidence.

"Everyone here is fighting against my odious principles. I have become an outcast. A terrible storm is gathering. But I should keep quiet. Like a beacon towering above an agitated sea, I shall smile while looking at my feet the useless waves' onslaughts. I have tried to enlighten my father, *Mirabile dictu!* He listened for a while to my arguments. He agrees with me about the impossibility of a direct influence of providence. He also agrees about the impossibility of the existence of witches, ghosts, and other legendary miracles. However, the moment I start to apply his beliefs and the very truths we had just wonderfully agreed upon, he jumps at me to impose silence with one unique argument, a perpetual theme as a matter of fact:

'I believe what I believe'. "On the other hand, my mother already sees me on the road to chaos and believes I want to pervert my sisters. This is so silly, really!"

Sadly, the home, previously full of joy during holidays, was saddened by this incident. Mr Timothy told his daughters to stop speaking to their brother and the littles ones appeared troubled by it. Nonetheless, as was habit, everyone got busy with Christmas preparations, even though no one was thrilled by it. They organised everything without any enthusiasm but with a forced gaiety, without the small surprises which are always so agreeable in a united family.

In secret, Elisabeth remained close to Shelley. Sadly, she realised that her own admiration ceased to be shared by her cousin Harriet, who appeared to her cold and more detached day by day.

Harriet had become exasperated by the many letters she received from Oxford, letters full of enthusiastic dissertations that were so difficult to follow. Quotes from Godwin annoyed her to the extreme, and worse, scared her.

Beautiful girls are seldom interested in dangerous ideas. Beauty, a natural form of order, is essentially conservative. It upholds established religion in being the ornamentation of its ceremonies; Venus has always been the best agent for Jupiter.

The beautiful Harriet showed the outrageous letters to her mother, and then to her father, who declared the ideas an abomination. Around her, all predicted a bad future for the young Shelley. Could one marry a rebel, whose follies alienated him from others?

Harriet liked elegance, balls and success. What would her life be like with this enthusiastic man who even did not respect marriage? And then, religion needed to be thought about.

Prior to Percy's arrival, the two young girls discussed the subject vehemently. Elisabeth was protecting her brother. How could Harriet compare self-interested satisfactions to the happiness of living by the side of this most wonderful man?

"You consider your brother as a remarkable being," Harriet replied. "However, how can I know that he is so? We have lived in the countryside; we do not know anything. Our parents, especially your father, Member of Parliament and with experience of people, is actually very critical of Percy's ideas. So, let's admit that he is genius. Then, have I got the right to start an intimate life with him, which will probably end up with disappointment when he realises how much I am inferior to the image his heated imagination has made of me? I am only a humble girl, very similar to others. He has idealised me. He could be quite surprised if he saw me as I am."

Such modesty was concerning, especially as one is not so rational about love. At Shelley's arrival, Elisabeth told him what Harriet said. He ran to her and found her as Elisabeth described her, cold and distant. She did not even ask him to exonerate himself; she only requested to be left alone. She rebuked him for being sceptical of everything.

"Harriet," Shelley said. "It is monstruous that I cannot own up to the convictions I have built from objective reasoning. In what way do my theological beliefs discredit me as a brother, a friend or even as a lover?"

"But," Harriet said, "you can think whatever you like, I just do not care. Do not ask me to link my destiny to yours."

It was the first time Shelley discovered feminine indifference, which always falls just like a dark night in the centre of Africa. He left, crazy with pain. Across the frozen forest, he came back slowly to Field-Place, and, without realising that everything was covered by snow, he went and paced up and down the village cemetery for most of the night. The cemetery was the scene of his young love. He came back home at around 2 in the night and went to bed. Before, he set up a pistol on the side of the bed and on the other side, various poisons from his chemical stores. However, the thought of Elisabeth's inevitable sadness on seeing his corpse prevented him from killing himself.

In the morning, he wrote to Hogg. He did not express any resentment about Harriet or Mr Timothy or even about Mr Grove. He felt that the only cause for this tragedy was intolerance itself. "My friend, I hereby swear to never forgive the intolerants. If I do not abide to this pledge, I ask to be punished by the infinite itself. In principle, I do not admit the idea of revenge. However, I accept it here only as legitimate. From now on, all my free time shall be dedicated to that mission. Intolerance ruins society itself, it triggers prejudices which often break the dearest and kindest connections. Oh! How much would I like to be the righter of wrongs, to be the one who could crush the Devil, who could hurl it down to its native inferno and then prevent it from coming back up. I would like to be the one who finally establishes universal tolerance.

"I hope to satisfy those hungry feelings, at least in my poetry. You shall see and recognise how the monster has hurt me. She is not mine anymore! She hates me as a sceptic, however, that is what she was once! Oh, zealotry! If I ever forgive its most recent persecution, if so, let the sky itself fall on me! (Of course, if the sky could ever be aware of the wrath itself)... Forgive me, my dear friend, I fear that there is some selfishness in this passionate love. I can feel too often that my soul itself is about to split. I wish I could escape passionate love; it is egocentric. I do not wish to have to lie for others… How much would I prefer to die in the struggle! Yes, that could be such a relief… Is suicide a crime? Last night, I slept all night close to my loaded pistol. If it were not for my sister, and but for you, I would have pronounced the final farewell."

There was only two weeks of holidays left. For Shelley, these were sad days at Field-Place, having to stay among an upset mother, a furious father and worried children. Harriet, despite several invitations from Elisabeth, refused to come back to Field-Place ever again. Well-informed people even talked about her engagement to an unknown person.

To calm his own pain with happiness for someone else, Shelley planned an engagement between his sister and his friend, disregarding the fact that they had actually never met. He sent to Hogg Elisabeth's poems, full of good intention and hatred for intolerance all mixed up with plenty of prosodic errors.

"All of us are brothers," wrote the good student Elisabeth. "All of us are brothers, even the African who bends under the strokes of the stick of the hard-hearted English man…" She had actually written a whole elegy in that style. In exchange, Shelley gave to her sister Hogg's poems, which he described as extremely beautiful, and where he himself was compared to a young oak, with Harriet Grove as ivy extinguishing the tree after having wrapped itself round.

"Though, you did not say," Shelley replied, "that the ivy, after having devastated the oak, then get around the nearby pine."

The nearby pine actually referred to Mr Heylar himself, a rich landowner and a man of sanctity, as if created by providence to escort his wife to the county's balls. "She is forever lost to me! She is married! Married to a piece of land! She will become, just like it, indifferent and raw matter. So many beautiful possibilities will vanish. Please, do not talk any more about this, my friend."

He would have liked to invite Hogg to be with them at Field-Place, for Elisabeth to judge by herself how admirable he was. However, Mr Timothy had not forgotten the warning of the editor about the bad angel. He simply forbade the invitation.

5
QUOD ERAT DEMONSTRANDUM

A month or so after that sad holiday, Mr Munday and Mr Slatter, the Oxford booksellers to whom Mr Timothy had recommended his son's literary fancies, saw young Shelley come in, his hair blowing in the wind and his shirt open. He was carrying a large bundle of pamphlets under his arm. He wanted them sold at sixpence each and displayed prominently in the window. To ensure it was done to his taste, he was going to do it himself.

Immediately, pushing aside the booksellers, he set to work. Amused, Mr Munday and Mr Slatter watched him bustling about with the fatherly and mocking benevolence that shopkeepers in university towns show to students well-endowed with pocket money. If they had looked more closely, they would have been terrified by the loads of explosive material that their young and aristocratic customer was piling up in elegant stacks in their honourable shop window. The title of the pamphlets was indeed the most scandalous that could be displayed in a theological and puritanical city: *The Necessity of Atheism*. They were signed by the unknown name of Jeremiah Stukeley, and if Mr Munday and Mr Slatter had leafed through them for a moment, they would have been even more appalled by the insolent logic of this imaginary Stukeley.

"Feelings are the origin of all knowledge." With this reckless axiom began the pamphlet, which, written in mathematical form, claimed to demonstrate the impossibility of the existence of God, and ended proudly with the three letters, QED: *quod erat demonstrandum*. To Shelley, who did not understand any mathematics, this was like a magic formula, like a modern incantation to evoke truth.

Although he was a fervent believer in the spirit of universal goodness, the creator and governor of all things, in the future life, and in a whole personal theology as an Anglican 'Savoyard Vicar', the word 'atheist' appealed to him because of its violence. He liked to throw it in the face of bigots. He picked up the word that had once been thrown at him at Eton, like a knight picks up a gauntlet. To the physical and moral courage that every good Englishman possesses, he claimed to add intellectual courage: the danger was great and the scandal inevitable. But like the fickle ivy wrapping itself around the neighbouring pine, intolerance had to be punished.

The Necessity of Atheism had been in print for only 20 minutes when the Reverend John Walker, a grim and inquisitive-looking man, an unofficial tutor at a mediocre college, passed by the shop and looked at the window.

"Necessity of Atheism! Necessity of Atheism! Necessity of Atheism!" read the Reverend, who, surprised, offended, indignant, entered the bookshop and said with authority:

"Mr Munday! Mr Slatter, what is the meaning of this?"

"Well, sir, we don't know. We have not read the publication..."

"'Necessity of Atheism'? That title alone should have alerted you..."

"Certainly, sir. Now that our attention has been drawn to that title..."

"Now that your attention has been drawn, Mr Munday and Mr Slatter, you will kindly remove all these copies from your shop window and any others you may possess, take them to your kitchen and burn them in your stove."

Mr Walker had no legal authority to give such orders. But the booksellers knew that all he had to do was to complain, and the students would then be banned from their shop. They bowed with an obsequious smile and sent the bookshop clerk to ask the young Percy Shelley to come and talk to them. "We're sorry, Mr Shelley, but the truth is we couldn't do otherwise. Mr Walker was absolutely insistent, and in your own interests..."

But self-interest was the least of Shelley's concerns. In his sharp, urgent voice, he claimed before the worried booksellers his right to think and to communicate his thoughts to others.

"Besides," he told them, "I have done better than to dangle my net in front of the old ignorant birds of Oxford. I have sent a copy of *The Necessity of Atheism* to all the English bishops, the Vice-Chancellor and the Masters of the Colleges, with the compliments of Jeremiah Stukeley, in my unconcealed handwriting."

* * *

A few days later an attendant came to Hogg's room to ask for Mr Shelley to report to the Dean at once. He went down to the college assembly room, where he found the Dean with a group of masters. It was a small group of teachers, both scholarly and puritan, unimaginative examples of industrious and classical Christianity, almost all of whom had long hated the young Shelley because of his long hair, his strange way of dressing and his truly vulgar taste for scientific experiments. The Dean showed a copy of *The Necessity of Atheism*, then asked him if he was the author. As the man spoke in a rough, insolent voice, Shelley did not reply.

"Are you or are you not the author of this book?"

"If you can prove it, give your evidence. It is neither fair nor legal to question me in that manner. These are the procedures of an inquisitor, not of free men in a free country."

"Do you deny that this is your work?"

"I shall not answer."

"In that case, you are expelled, and I want you to leave this college tomorrow morning at the latest."

An envelope sealed with the college stamp was immediately handed to him by one of the assessors. It contained the expulsion order.

Shelley ran to Hogg's room, dropped down on the sofa and repeated, shaking with rage: 'Expelled! Expelled!' His teeth were chattering. The sanction was terrible indeed. It meant the interruption of all his studies, the impossibility of resuming them at another university, the certain deprivation of the beautiful, quiet life he loved, and the expected lasting buffoonish fury of his father.

Hogg was shocked and indignant too. Carried away by an imprudent friendship, he wrote a note on the spot expressing his sorrow and astonishment that such treatment could have been inflicted on such a gentleman. He hoped that the sanction would not be final.

A servant was asked to deliver this message to the Dean and his assembly of Masters, which was still in session. He returned immediately to bring Hogg the Dean's order to go downstairs. The hearing was short. "Did you write this?" It was the note Hogg had just sent, and he recognised it.

"And what about this pamphlet?"

With great courage and the skills of an old lawyer, Hogg explained the absurdity of the question, the injustice of having condemned Shelley and the obligation of every man conscious of his rights...

"Well, you are expelled!" replied the Dean with anger.

He was clearly in the mood to expel the whole college that evening. Hogg in turn received a sealed envelope.

In the afternoon, a notice was placed on the doors of the Hall. It gave the names of the two culprits and announced that they were being publicly expelled for refusing to answer the questions put to them.

6
TIMOTHY SHELLEY'S VIGOROUS DIALECTIC

The outcasts left Oxford in a coach. While waiting news from his father, Shelley borrowed £20 from the booksellers to help him to settle and live in London.

Most of the rooms he and Hogg visited seemed unsuitable for living really: the street was too noisy, the borough too dirty or the maid too ugly. However and at last, Poland Street appealed to Shelley, as it triggered some pleasant associations in his mind… "Poland, Warsaw, freedom". Only rooms worthy of free men could exist in Poland Street, he thought.

Indeed, the first room they found was wallpapered in a blue and green grape pattern and appeared to them as one of the most beautiful rooms in the entire world.

"This is it," said Shelley. "This should be our home for ever. We shall resume our daily activities just like in Oxford: lectures at the fireside, walks, experiences. We shall pass our life here."

This was a delightful plan, for which, however, the agreement of Mr Timothy and Mr Hogg senior were both missing.

* * *

When Mr Timothy heard of the events at Oxford, he became quite upset and furious. As a renowned landowner as well as a Member of Parliament and as a court judge for his county, the situation and the resulting disapprobation became particularly risky. Most importantly, the accusation of atheism was bothering him. Indeed, he was known to be a liberal, a boldness in politics which nonetheless required some degree of religious orthodoxy on his part.

So, he wrote a letter full of solemnity to Mr Hogg and complained about "the sad Oxford situation which involved both my son and yours". He begged him to recall as soon as possible "his young man". "And for me," he added, "I shall recommend to mine to read, as a minimum requirement, *Natural Theology or Evidences of the Existence and Attributes of the Deity* by Paley. This book should suit his case. I shall even read it with him."

He then composed for "his young man" a harsh and powerful letter: "Despite that I could, as a father, suffer the shame of you as the result of your criminal ideas, I have strict duties in face of my Christian feelings, but also in the face of your young brothers and sisters and my own reputation. If you still wish to get help, assistance and protection from me, you must:

1. Immediately come back to Field-Place and refrain from any contact whatsoever with Mr Hogg.

2. Be placed under the direction of gentlemen I shall select for that purpose."

If those conditions were not to be accepted, Mr Timothy would simply abandon his son to misery even if, in reality, this tended to fit with his diabolical ideas.

The reply was short: "My dear father, as you honourably asked my intentions to serve the determination of your conduct, I feel it is my duty (even though it upsets me to hurt your feelings concerning both your own reputation and that of your family) to simply reject both proposals written in your letter and to confirm that such a refusal shall continue indefinitely to apply to any other such request. With all my thanks for your goodwill, I remain your kind and respectful son, Percy Shelley."

* * *

The great difficulty of a father's diplomacy is the very fact that as a negotiator he wishes with all his power to avoid a total breakdown of relations. This renders any sanctions difficult to apply. With his 'conditions' curtly rejected; Mr Timothy was at a loss.

He was not a bad man, though. He trusted the power of dialectic from a port bottle. He so decided to go to London and invited the rebels to the Miller Hotel, where the wine was known to be good.

While awaiting the two outcasts, he thought that in the end, one must take children with good heart… Even so, one must, however ridiculous it appears, have a serious conversation with them… A mature and thoughtful mind can always reason without difficulty an 18-year-old philosopher, and great evils can be prevented with a discussion to the point …. In any case, Percy was the heir of the domain, it is to him that the title of the Shelley family shall be passed: therefore, it was necessary to bring him back to reason.

The kind Mr Timothy rubbed his hands with some satisfaction while, in his mind, turning and turning Paley's theological arguments.

At the same time, the two young people walked from Poland Street while joking and reading out Voltaire's *Philosophical Dictionary*. Shelley, particularly, savoured with interest what the old Frenchman said about Jewish people, the intolerance found in the Bible and about Jehovah's cruelty.

When they arrived at the hotel, Mr Timothy was with Mr Graham, the secretary working for the Shelley family. With hypocritical goodwill, Mr Timothy welcome Hogg, then, addressing his son, point-blank started a long discourse which ended up being incomprehensible and punctuated by drama. It was perceived as ridiculous by the younger men. Shelley leaned towards his friend and murmured:

"So, what do you think of my father?"

"He is not your father," Hogg whispered, "he is Jehovah himself."

Shelley laughed loudly.

"What's the matter, Shelley? Are you sick?" said Mr Timothy with outrage. "Are you mad? Why are you laughing?"

Fortunately, just at that moment, dinner was announced. As the meal proved to be excellent, the conversation became somewhat cordial. When dessert was put on the table, Mr Timothy sent his son to order horses and took the opportunity to attempt to conquer Hogg.

"Sir, you are actually very different from what I expected… You seem to me an agreeable gentleman, humble and reasonable… So, tell me. What do you think I should do for my poor boy? He is mad, is he not?"

"A little, yes, sir."

" So, what do you think I should do?"

"If he had married his cousin, he would have changed. He needs someone to care for him, a good woman. Why not marry him?"

"But how? This is impossible! If I propose him a young woman, he will certainly refuse; I know him."

"He would refuse only if you were ordering him to marry, and I would agree with him. However, if you were connecting him with a well-chosen young lady, it is possible she would appeal to him. Furthermore, if the first choice did not work, you could try someone else."

Mr Graham agreed this could be a magnificent plan indeed. And so the two men started to write on the table corner a list of potential young ladies, when Shelley came back. Mr Timothy asked for a bottle of old port and started to selfishly praise himself. He was much respected at the Parliament, by all the members but most importantly by the speaker, who told him once: "Mr Shelley, I do not know what we would do without you." He carried on saying that he was very much appreciated in Sussex, his county as an excellent high court judge. He then told a long story about two poachers he had condemned. "Graham, you remember those two, don't you?" Graham agreed. He then said, "When they got out of jail, they came to thank me."

Hogg never found out why these two poor men would have thanked a merciless judge, because at that very moment, judging the readiness for port, Mr Timothy tackled the essential subject.

"I think," he said, "there is certainly a god… Any doubt about is simply and utterly impossible."

None of the listeners expressed any doubt whatsoever.

"You, sir," he said, turning towards Hogg. Have you got any personal doubt?"

"Not at all, sir."

"Because, if you had any, I could prove to you the very existence of God, in just one minute."

"But, sir, I have none."

"Al right! … However, would you like to listen to my argument?"

"Yes, with pleasure."

"Good, I shall read it to you."

He checked his pockets, took out letters, bills, and at the end a piece of paper and then started to read. Shelley, leaning forward, listened with great attention.

"I have already heard this," he said after a few moments; and turning towards Hogg, said, "Where have I listened to this before?"

"But," Hogg said, "this is Paley's argument!"

"Exactly," said the reader with satisfaction, "you are correct: those are the arguments of Paley. I have just this morning copied this from his book. However, Paley got those very arguments from me; the whole of Paley's book is indeed from me."

And so, he folded the piece of paper, put it back in his pocket, rather disappointed.

His son was looking at him with even more contempt than ever, and the dinner ended without bringing any sign of reconciliation. Shelley refused to follow his father, and his father refused to give him any money. The only two people who left quite happy with each other were Hogg and Mr Timothy. Mr Timothy found his son's friend more human than Percy, who was most of the time, dishevelled, tense and on the defensive. He always backed principles which one could not criticise without hurting his pride. On the other hand, at such a young age, Hogg seemed to already understand life. His idea of marriage made perfect sense.

Later, Hogg commented that although the Member of Parliament was quite verbose, he was easy-going and certainly welcoming.

A few days later, Hogg proved again that he understood life in making peace with his own father, who, as the head of an old conservative family well known for the exactitude of its religious beliefs, did not need, unlike the liberal lord of Field-Place, to demonstrate the horror of the activities of his own young man.

He advised to his son to study law and found a placement for him in a law firm in York. As a result, Hogg had to abandon Shelley in the room on Poland Street, all alone and surrounded by green and blue grapes.

7
AN ACADEMY FOR YOUNG LADIES

Left alone in London, without any friends, any job or money, Shelley just fell into despair. He passed days in his room writing melancholic verses and letters to Hogg. In the evening, not knowing what to do next, he was in bed by 8. Sleeping became the only way for him to stop endlessly telling himself about his misfortune. As soon as he was half-dreaming though, the image of his beautiful and unfaithful cousin came to his mind to torture him. He tried to tackle the painful visions with syllogisms.

"I used to love a being," he said to himself. "However, the soul of this very being is not what it was before. As such, the being is not anymore, because I loved its soul and not its body. I could as well talk about love to the worms which shall one day appear by the side of the previously beloved's corpse in the horror of the ossuary".

This type of reasoning appeared to him good, yet he was perplexed. Actually, it did not comfort him at all.

Financial issues were getting worse by the day. Mr Timothy had not contacted him. One day, out of the blue, they both met in London. Shelley addressed his father politely: "Are you well?" In reply, he received a look as dark as a stormy sky together with a majestic: "Your humble servant, Sir."

Fortunately, his sisters did not forget about him. They sent him their own pocket money; this was all he had to live on. At Field-Place, Elisabeth was under scrutiny, however the two youngest boarded at the academy of young girls run by Mrs Fenning in Clapham. The students soon discovered the beautiful eyes, the open shirt and the unruly curls of Helen Shelley's brother.

He arrived with pockets full of raisins and biscuits and started to talk about universal themes in front of a circle of delighted little girls. Of course, he decided to 'enlighten' the prettiest ones. He could not bear that these beautiful faces should be abandoned to 'prejudice'.

Most importantly, he admired the fair hair and the delicate rosy skin of his sisters' best friend, the charming Harriet Westbrook. She was 16 years old, petite but beautifully built, with a naturally joyful and deliciously fresh air. She became very useful when Mrs Fenning (under the request of Mr Timothy) asked for fewer visits. Harriet, whose parents lived in London, was going in and out daily; it was to her that the sisters' money and cakes were given. And so, the Poland Street hermit became her great friend.

Harriet Westbrook's father had previously owned a coffee shop. He wanted his daughter to have the education of a grandee's daughter. Following the death of her mother, Harriet had been looked after by her sister, Eliza, who was already a fairly mature young woman.

One can imagine how much the Westbrook family would have been interested by the son of a baronet, heir of a huge wealth and furthermore as beautiful as a god, who was living in all simplicity in a small room on bread and dry figs, to whom the youngest of the Westbrooks was bringing his sisters' pocket money to prevent him starving to death.

Eliza insisted on going to visit the hero. Harriet brought her along on one of her expeditions. At first, the former coffee shop owner's oldest daughter frightened Shelley. She was dry and skinny. Her white face seemed tarnished by scars, and her two blank eyes were like gazing without any wit at all; and worse, a mass of black hair topped the whole thing.

Miss Eliza Westbrook was quite proud of her hair, though. Her affected manner contrasted sharply that of with her young sister, whose laughter attested her simplicity. However, Shelley quickly forgot his first impressions when he saw that this older woman was showing clear signs of friendship towards him. Not only that. The eldest sister did not object to Harriet's visits, as one might have feared, but instead, offered to chaperone her sister. On several occasions, she even invited Shelley for dinner, when

Mr Westbrook was out, of course. Furthermore, Eliza won the heart of the young philosopher in asking to be enlightened too. She started reading *The Philosophical Dictionary* under his direction.

Harriet's daily walks in the company of Shelley attracted the attention of the academy of young women. One of the teachers told her off with some words of caution: "This young Mr Shelley is known for his rebellious ideas; it is likely that his morality is no better than his ideas, you know."

One of Harriet's letters, full of dangerous reasoning, was seized. She was then referred to as the atheist's friend and was threatened with being expelled. All the gentlemen's daughters started to ignore the coffee shop owner's daughter, and life at school became very difficult indeed.

One day, as Shelley was reading by the fireplace, Eliza sent a messenger to inform him that his companion was sick and expressly asked him to come and attend her. He went and found Harriet in bed, very pale, but more beautiful than ever with her chestnut hair loose. Mr Westbrook went upstairs to say goodnight to Shelley, who was quite embarrassed by the situation. Whatever his horror of prejudices, this evening visit to a young woman's bedroom appeared to him to be quite intrusive in all honesty. Mr Westbrook was amicable though, very amicable: "I am sorry I cannot be with you; I have got friends downstairs; if you wish to join us later, you are welcome…" Shelley was thankful, but Mr Westbrook's friends had no attraction to him really.

He sat down by Harriet's bed, close to Eliza, who eloquently talked at length about love. Suddenly, Harriet complained of a sharp headache and said she could not stand anymore the noise of conversation. "I will leave and go downstairs," Eliza said, leaving the two children. Shelley stayed until half-past midnight, while Mr Westbrook and his friends were laughing and drinking downstairs.

The next day, Harriet got better.

* * *

Since he could visit young women and enlighten their spirits, even in exile, Shelley's sadness lessened. However, he still suffered from the separation from his sister, Elisabeth. When she stopped responding to his letters, he wondered if she ended up being locked down. He wished he could go back to Field-Place to see her, whatever the difficulties. Sometimes, he thought about going back the 'American' way. What would happen, if one night, without alerting anyone, he went and settled back there while reacting only with silence to Mr Timothy's curses? However, it all became more positive when Mrs Shelley's brother, Captain Pilfold, intervened and offered a badly needed jumping-off place for his nephew to tackle Field-Place.

Captain Pilfold was an old mariner, brave, hearty and jovial, who commanded under Nelson a frigate in Trafalgar. He preferred a hundred times his fanciful nephew over Timothy, his brother-in-law, who was too full of solemnity. The captain did not care if Percy was a sceptic or not. The child had will, and this was the most important feature of his character. So, he invited him to visit him at Cuckfield, 10 miles from Field-Place. He received Shelley with grandeur, who, in return proposed to 'enlighten' him.

The captain proved to be such a good student that after eight days, he surprised both the clergyman and the doctor of the village with incendiary syllogisms.

There, Shelley met the local teacher, Miss Hitchener, who was a rather beautiful girl with a Roman nose. She was around 30 years of age and a republican. In the village, she had the reputation for being both glamorous and patronising. On her side, she used to complain of being misunderstood. Shelley, after having understandably admired the nobility of her attitude, realised with sadness that she was still a deist. And so, as usual, he offered to start writing to her with the purpose of curing her of this handicap. She agreed.

Meanwhile, Captain Pilfold, with determination, prepared a plan to tackle his brother-in-law. He had the genius idea of enrolling for this enterprise the Duke of

Norfolk himself, who happened to be the political chief of the liberal party. Snobbishness won over paternal vanity. Shelley was able to go back to Field-Place with all the honours of war; he was even rewarded an unconditional annual pension of £200 sterling.

* * *

Finally, Shelley could see his sister, Elisabeth. However, He was surprised to find her so different. She was more joyful, livelier than ever before, but with an incredible triviality. He used to know her as serious, enthusiastic; he found her indifferent towards ideas, only bothered by trivial occupations, balls and stupid conversations. She was now living only for the high society.

He tried, like before, to share Hogg's letters.

"Oh! You and your absurd friend!... All my acquaintances believe you are both mad."

And then she started to talk about marriage; as a matter of fact, she thought only about this subject. Nothing more horrific could upset Shelley. Had she actually forgotten their past reading about the pure ideas of Godwin?

"Marriage is hateful and simply odious," he replied. "I feel nauseated when I think of this horrific chain, which is the heaviest one mankind has forged to fasten proud souls. Scepticism and free love are as necessarily connected as religion and marriage are. Honourable people have no need of law… For God's sake, Elisabeth, read over the marriage service, and see for yourself if an honest man can submit himself to a loving and loved person with such aggravation."

"However, you still wish that I marry Hogg, do you not?"

"Yes, but not in front of a clergyman, or according to the law of men; but freely with love itself as the higher priest."

"Here is the advice you give to a sister, Percy!" Elisabeth said with contempt.

It was useless to try and convince a spirit which had become so superficial with no possible cure. "Why would I deceive myself? She is lost, completely lost. Intolerance has infected her. She just talks about conventions and trivial stupidities. What would she wish from me? To be a beater in a husband hunting? No, never!"

He had gone back to Field-Place only to see Elisabeth again. Even so, he just had to leave. Invitations were not lacking; Captain Pilfold would happily welcome him at Cuckfield; Mr Westbrook begged him to join him and his daughters for a family holiday in the mountains; Hogg asked him to stay with him for a month in York. It was there, actually, where he was most tempted to go. However, Mr Timothy, who attached a symbolical importance to the separation of the two Oxford criminals, would have been upset of the possibility of a new coming together and, since the first quarter of the allowance would be payable on 1st

September, it was certainly wise to be patient. Hogg wrote in a pleasant tone that anyway it was likely that the pretty Harriet Westbrook's invitation would win over an old friend. "Your jokes amuse me," Shelley replied. "If I have just a tiny idea of what love is, I do not love anyone at the moment. However, I have heard from the Westbrooks, both of whom I highly esteem".

As he still hesitated on the way to take, one of his mother's cousins offered him hospitality in a remote corner of Wales: it was a way for him to save money while waiting for his pension, he accepted.

Crossing London, he was hoping to see Miss Hitchener and have lunch with her. However, the teacher with the Roman profile feared it was somewhat inappropriate: their respective statuses were too inequal! Shelley, upset by this very idea, wrote a beautiful letter about equality where Miss Hitchener was referred as "the sister of his soul". She began to think that, after all, Lady Shelley was a nice name and started to stare at herself in mirrors.

8
THIS HORRIFIC CHAIN

The countryside in Wales was wild and beautiful. The barren rocks, plunging torrents and woody gorges enchanted Shelley. Often, he went to sit down near some shady waterfalls and read his friends' letters. He felt like the master of numerous 'souls': Miss Hitchener, the trusty Hogg, Captain Pilfold (now dreaded by the bigoted), Eliza and Harriet Westbrook, and without counting several unknown individuals.

The Westbrooks had just gone back to London when Shelley received the gloomiest and most concerning letter from Harriet. Her father wanted to force her to return to the school of Mrs Fenning, where she had been so sad. The students were avoiding talking to her and even not replying to any of her requests. The teachers considered her a lost girl. Rather than staying in this jail, she was prepared to kill herself. "Why living? Nobody likes me and I have no one to love. Is suicide a crime for a useless being to others and unbearable to itself? Since there is no divine law, can the human law forbid such a natural act?"

Shelley was grabbed by a kind of terror. His student's logic seemed to him irreproachable. His own teaching had made this student. However, could he coldly reply and abandon her to death? Before her despair, she could have struggled and refused to obey. He advised her to be firm and wrote to Mr Westbrook a letter of complaint.

The old café shop owner was offended. Why on earth was this aristocrat, who, for the past six months, had been around his daughters was now getting involved? Eliza had suggested that at some point Shelley might ask Harriet to be his wife. However, have we ever seen a baronet marry a café shop owner's daughter? This Sir Shelley was certainly looking for some other advantage than marriage. Anyway, he had made up his mind the night when, in his daughter's bedroom, he had invited him to join his friends. Sir Shelley declined his offer with contempt; he remembered. Friend of the people? Egalitarian? The very grandson of Sir Bysshe Shelley, a millionaire? Whatever, these people were all the same.

An order to leave was given to Harriet.

She wrote a last letter to Shelley about a less gloomy plan compared with the previous suicidal project. Still, she was very sad, much persecuted and ready to flee with him, if this was agreeable.

Without waiting, in great turmoil, he took the coach for London. It was unquestionable that he had duties towards this child. He had educated her; he had contributed to the building of a courageous soul now seemingly unable to tolerate injustice. He remembered that a letter from him was the initial trigger of her disapprobation. However, if he were to flee with her, how would they live? Where? He had no profession, no future. In any case, did he actually love her? Was he still able to love, following his recent separation?

Harriet was a charming person and the idea of a voyage in the company of the pretty sick woman he had seen that evening, with loose hair was just intoxicating. It became rather difficult not to visualise such delicious images.

Finally, he saw her. She was skinny, very pale, quite tragic.

"And so, has one made you suffer so much?

"No, no, my friend, but…" She was hesitating and said: " I love you…" Her pallor, her eyes fixed on Shelley, her emotions, all said enough. The truth was that she was madly in love with him. This little girl had literally been transformed by him. Before knowing him, she had normal tastes for her social background. She used to admire the red costumes of the soldiers, and when she thought about love, her heroes had a military connection. However, when she thought of marriage, she was imagining a clergyman. Shelley was a complete departure from such usual dreams of young girls. When she had first heard about his ideas on religion and politics, she was frightened and promised herself she would convert him. However, Shelley's logic crushed hers from their first dialogue. Intimidated by a stronger mind, she felt humiliated with delight and subsequently adored the man and his doctrine.

Realising that he may be undecided about joining her, she had feared she would never see him again and exaggerated her suffering to make her hero run to her.

Shelley never admired the knights-errant; he did not consider their conduct rational. It seemed harsh to him to give to a woman a life that could be dedicated to humanity. However, in front of this beautiful and anxious face, knowing his words could paint it with happiness, he forgot about his principles. He offered his hand to Harriet and declared that he was completely hers. Still, with some prudence, he rejected the idea of an immediate escape: speeding up the situation seemed to him unnecessary and even dangerous. In case anyone was tempted to hurt her, she could call him; wherever he was, and he would run to collect her. She regained the healthy colour of a sixteen-year-old who knows she is beloved.

* * *

As soon as he left the room, when out of sight of the young girl, Shelley sighed deeply and fell into a deep meditative mode.

He wrote to Hogg about the situation. Hogg replied bluntly, supplicating his friend not to escape with Harriet without marrying her. Despite his knowledge of Shelley's disagreement with marriage, he tried some powerful arguments: "If you do not marry her, who will be at risk? You or her? Only her, certainly; it shall be her who will be hated; it shall be her who will sacrifice not only her reputation but her safety. Have you got the right to impose on her such a situation?"

The argument was smart. Selfishness was the attitude Shelley hated the most. However, he still felt he could commit a shameful and immoral act by getting married. The chapters in *Political Justice* against the 'marital chains' were bothering him. At that moment, somebody told him that Godwin himself had married twice, and this reassured him. "Yes," he replied to Hogg, "it is indeed useless to hope with one unique example to renew the shape of society, until reason has produced a complete change and the cessation of exposure to numerous wrongs."

However, he was not in a hurry to apply his new ideas. His uncle Pilfold called him to come to Cuckfield. He was aware that he would see again the beautiful teacher with the Roman profile, "sister of my soul". He wished to resume her initiation into the doctrine. On leaving, he promised Harriet he would come back to London at her first demand.

Only a 19-year-old could not conceive any doubt about what would happen next. A loving young woman, who knows she is armed with a promise, just cannot resist for long. Even before the end of the week, an urgent message requested Shelley back to London. The tormentors wanted yet again to abandon Andromeda to the scholarly dragon.

Shelley saw no other solution. He offered to flee with Harriet and to get married with immediate effect.

The next day, the coach to Edinburgh carried north these two children, who between them had only 35 years of life. "An act of will, not of passion," thought the young knight, while settled in the high-speed coach, bounced about in front of his delicious, betrothed beauty.

9
CHILDLIKE COUPLE

A couple of young lovers, charming but persecuted, are irresistibly attractive. Edinburgh's inhabitants, who are not known to be sentimental, especially when money is concerned, could not but welcome with tolerant amusement this childish couple who came to them in such dire straits. On leaving London, Shelley had borrowed some money from a friend; on arriving in Edinburgh, not a penny was left. It was pointless to seek help from Mr Timothy, who was probably furious about his son's escape.

However, one landlord agreed to rent them an agreeable ground floor apartment on three conditions: they would tell him and his friends about their adventure, he would be able to glimpse Harriet's beauty, and they would promise rapid repayment. He did even more. He lent them enough money not only to eat over the next few days, but to celebrate their marriage according to Scottish law. His only further condition was that, on the evening of the wedding, Shelley and his wife should share their dinner with him and his friends.

And so, it happened. The grandson of Sir Bysshe Shelley celebrated his wedding amid Edinburgh's shop owners. The wine, together with the spectacle of these two young spouses, made the honest puritans a little too smutty for Shelley's taste. The jokes became inadequate. The pretty Harriet, who was modest, blushed a lot. Shelley announced that he and his wife would retire to their bedroom. A roar of laugher was the reply.

Sometimes later, someone knocked at the door. Shelley opened it: it was their host. "It is traditional here," he said, a little bit drunk, "that the guests at a wedding go up during the night to wash the bride in whisky."

"I shall blow the brain of anyone trespassing this door!" said Shelley, showing off his pistols.

His voice trembled, his eyes sparkled, just like before at Eton. And so, the traders decided that this young man with a girl's face was in fact more dangerous than he looked. Respectfully, they wished him a good night and went downstairs in a hurry.

This is how Shelley and Harriet got married, free and all alone in a strange large city. They looked at each other with delight.

A few days were enough for the young husband, who, in the stage to Edinburgh, had thought with melancholia: "An act of will, not of passion" to fall in love. Harriet was certainly agreeable to admire, always pretty, fresh and vivid, her hair always well done, without a single wild lock. She looked just like a pink and white flower. She used to dress simply but always neatly. Without being knowledgeable, she was remarkably educated. Essentially, she had read numerous books. She was reading all day, and furthermore read moral books by choice.

Her master and lover communicated to her the required respect for virtue. Fenelon's Telemachus became her favourite hero. She often tried to spell out the magical words, "Intolerance, equality, justice", and her childish mouth ended up pronouncing views which would have offended the Lord Chancellor himself. In regard to the Anglican religion, she simply ignored it as gullibly in the manner of Calypso and Nausicaa.

Children are delightful, but their company can be tiring. Even though Shelley was affected by such grace, kindness and devotion, he happened to miss the caustic conversation with Hogg and the eloquent enthusiasm of Miss Hitchener. He was wondering with concern what her thoughts were about his marriage.

"My dear friend," he wrote to her. "Can I still refer to you that way, or have I lost the esteem of a wise and virtuous being with my equivocal behaviour? All my projects have changed so much in just one week. How often one gets enslaved by circumstances! …You are probably wondering, how, I, as an atheist, could have submitted myself to a wedding. How could my conscience have abdicated and accepted? This is what I wish to explain to you." Then, following Hogg's previous thinking, he demonstrated that good reputation and benefits depend to each other's and that they should both be essentially protected by the loved one. "Criticise me, if you wish, my dearest friend, because you are still the best in my eyes! If Harriet is not at 16 who you are with your advanced age, would you help me to train in everything this noble soul which deserves your care… Charming, she is already, unless I am the weakest of error's slaves." The letter finished with an invitation to come and join them in Edinburgh, where the very presence of Harriet would prevent any ill-appropriateness of their meeting. Miss Hitchener did not accept.

It is likely that the poetic, familiar tone did not suffice to make acceptable the inappropriate phrase that juxtaposed 16 years old and a more 'advanced age'.

Even if the virgin of Cuckfield did not come to help and model Harriet's soul, Shelley, hearing one morning someone knocking at the window of his ground floor rooms, rejoiced in seeing in the street, standing holding a bag, his old friend Hogg, who was coming to pass a few weeks in Edinburgh, after being given some holidays from the law firm in York.

Hogg was welcomed triumphantly. "Finally, we are together! We should never again leave one another! We must prepare you a bed in the house." Harriet appeared; Hogg was shocked. Never ever before had he seen a woman with such sparkling youth, beauty and happiness. The owner was forcibly called upon. "We need another bed! With immediate effect please! Another bed in this home, this is urgent and essential…" The man replied and offered a room in the attic.

The three friends had so much to talk about; everybody was talking at the same time. A tiny maid brought some tea, amid loud shouting. When the joy calmed down, Shelley suggested a walk to visit Mary Stuart's palace. Harriet, as a good student of the young ladies' academy and a big reader of historical novels, started to explain in detail many interesting facts. Upon leaving the palace, Shelley apologised. He needed to go and write some letters. However, he asked Harriet to guide Hogg up the famous hill, from which one could see the whole town.

Hogg admired at length the view, and both stayed a while at the top. His guide was pleasing him so much that he found the walk just delightful.

Going down, Harriet realised that the violent wind was lifting her skirts and that Hogg, in secret, glimpsed at her ankles. She sat down on the rock and declared that she would not move from it until the wind ceased. Hogg, who was starting to feel hungry, disagreed and left on his own. She ran and followed him. It is so that a few delightful weeks started.

Money was the only worry, even if the brave Pilfold was often sending gifts, "To be furious against one's son is fine," he said, "but to starve him is another matter." Hogg was getting some money of his own too and this despite Mr Timothy writing to his father, "I believe it is my duty to alert you that my good young man flew to Scotland with a young person of the opposite sex and that your son has joined them."

Every morning, Shelley was going out to collect his letters, the number of which was increasing. After breakfast, he was writing or working on a translation of Buffon. Harriet and Hogg were going out for walks. If the weather was bad, Harriet would read out loud to Hogg. She actually liked reading out loud very much and was good at it, her enunciation being of high quality. Hogg listened in such a way to Telemachus in its near entirety, and yet, never complained. The wise Idomeneus enunciating laws in Crete was very boring, however, the narrator was so pretty that he could have listened to it day after day without complaining. Shelley, less polite, sometimes fell asleep. His friend joined his wife in telling him off with comical reproaches. Hogg, without thinking, took pleasure in joining up with Harriet.

We were in 1811, the year of the comet and a fine vintage. The nights were translucent and sparkled.

10
WHO WAS HOGG?

Since Hogg's holiday was nearly ending and he needed to go back to his work in York, Shelley and Harriet, who did not have anything to do in Edinburgh, or indeed in any other place in the world, decided to follow him. In front of them, a plan was developing, one that was simple but necessary. So they would stay in York with their friend until he finished his training, then the three of them would go to London to live forever, writing, reading and narrating to each other.

To prevent Harriet becoming tired, they hired a post-chaise. From both sides of the road, barley and beetroot fields alternated with monotony.

"But, where is the barley? Where are the beetroots?" Harriet asked.

"Eh, little town girl!" Shelley replied, infuriated.

Hogg, the tease, was asking himself how on earth the wise Idomeneus, so knowledgeable in agriculture, had not instructed his student yet.

To distract the travellers on their lengthy journey, Harriet kept reading out loud Telemachus, while Shelley sighed deeply: "Harriet darling, is it necessary to read it all?

"Certainly, yes."

"Could you skip some of it?"

" No, that is simply impossible."

At the first stop Shelley disappeared. He always had the astonishing power to disappear in thin air, just like an elf. Hogg found him at the seaside; he was watching the setting sun, looking quite melancholic.

He disliked York at first sight. The religious and civilised grandeur of the old capital of the North could not touch him. Furthermore, they could only find miserable rooms. "We cannot stay there," Shelley insisted.

However, to leave, he needed money. He so decided to visit the brave captain Pilfold, the defender of good people. From there, he could go back to York, passing through London to collect Eliza for a visit much desired by Harriet. The reunion of all Shelley's spiritual sisters could finally happen.

He therefore took the coach; Harriet and Hogg were left together, all alone. It was a peculiar but a delightful situation. In the foreign town, they felt as free as on a desert island. Harriet played childishly at running the house with her young and amusing companion. Hogg's sarcastic tone amused her, as it contrasted with Shelley's fervent seriousness, even though she admired her lover so much. Hogg complimented her a thousand times. She did not find this ridiculous, on the contrary. In her eyes, Percy remained partly 'the schoolmaster'; he taught her what she knew; he corrected with seriousness her mistakes; he knew her talents.

Hogg, on the other hand, admired everything. He took notice of her dresses and of her hair. He listened to Telemachus while complimenting the voice of the narrator. He was always in a good mood. That was simply delightful.

Hogg's state of mind was different and less naive. Living all day with such a charming young lady, he began to desire her with a passion. Shelley himself had left him to stay with her, and her own family may have not educated her to keep reserved and on guard in such circumstances. At first, he decided it was a horrible thought to desire her to such an extreme, and that the much-loved spouse of a friend could not be a woman for himself. However, wit can work like a procuress, and his vivid wit worked in the service of his revelling instincts.

"Is that my fault?" he thought, "if Shelley throws her in my arms? How can one think of writing letters about virtue, when one has in his own home such a wonder? For, she is just ravishing. When she walks York's streets, even the pharisee goes and watches her from the windows… In any case, does Shelley love her, really? He is treating her with affection and is very protective, yet to some extent, he seems detached, and I do not blame him…. What is Harriet? The daughter of a café shop owner…She should not be too difficult."

Since his first meeting with Shelley, he had been in two minds. He admired his moral courage, his friend's frankness and his raging loyalty. He recognised in his soul a pure and unique diamond. However, at the same time, his scepticism noticed the naivety of such fervent clamours and the feverish activity which seemed to achieve nothing. At Oxford, he used to be the cultured Sancho, the humanist mocking this Don Quixote with blond curls; with him, he got beaten by windmills. At the start of their friendship and until their reunion in Edinburgh, his admiration for Shelley was captivating, his mockery only coloured his champion competitor's behaviour with tender reflection. But now, the irony, triggered by this new illicit passion, was growing by the day.

On the first day of Shelley's absence, he invited Harriet for a walk to the riverside. He was looking at her with delight, while telling her a thousand follies. She talked about her husband and her impatient wait for his return; she talked about seeing him again, and of course about her sister, Eliza, who shall be with Shelley at his return. "Eliza is beautiful, you will see; she has beautiful black hair; she is clever…Eliza has always guided me at the time of important moments of my life…"

"And so, little girl, you have already had important moments in your life?"

Harriet then told him about her difficulties at school, her wedding; she then became silent, like busy remembering. Then she said: "What are your thoughts in regard to suicide? Have you ever thought of killing yourself?"

"Never," said Hogg. "And you, I hope...?"

"O no, often I have thought about it... even at school. Sometimes, I woke up at night with the idea of killing myself. I looked through the window... I bade farewell to the moon, the stars and to the sleeping students... And then, and then, I went back to sleep."

They kept on walking while exchanging secrets. Then, they decided to go back at home for tea, a time when Hogg was always amusing. After tea, Harriet proposed reading out loud. Hogg did not remember what she read on that night. But, at the moment she retired to her bedroom and gently said "Goodnight" he thought: "Could she be delightful, could she?"

The next day, as soon as he saw her, he told her that he was madly in love with her.

Harriet was shocked. This little girl of only 16, stood up for herself quite well. She started to speak about Shelley, about being virtuous, and then said: "Can't you see how terrible your behaviour is? Percy entrusted you to protect me, and then you abuse his confidence... However, I know you are already regretting it... I ask you not to say anything more about it... nor will I say anything to Shelley, who trusts you so much!"

She became animated while talking. A love declaration is always the start of a battle for any beautiful woman, yet a good soldier does not dislike the fight. This time, the courageous Harriet wan; Hogg swore to be well-behaved.

In the evening, when he was back from the law firm, he saw, sitting on the sofa, close to Harriet, a tall woman with hair as dark as a raven and with a pallid face and a horse-like look. "Hogg," said Harriet, "this is Eliza… She has come to visit: it is so nice of her, is it not? Eliza, this is Hogg, our great friend Shelley has talked to us so much about."

Eliza coldly tilted her head: "I thought you were supposed to travel with Shelley?" said Hogg.

"O! Dear, no!" said Eliza. She then went back talking with Harriet, without taking any notice of the newcomer. Hogg was not used to such treatment in this house. "Is this Eliza?" he thought. "She is awful and rude… Here is the end of my flirtation with Harriet… This may be better… however, the situation is quite despicable… "Darling Harriet," he said loudly, are we having tea? Are you not having tea, Miss Westbrook?" he said politely, turning towards Eliza.

"O! Dear, no!" Eliza said.

"What about you, Harriet?"

"Me neither."

Resigned, Hogg made himself some tea and drank it silently, all alone.

From that moment, the home became unbearable to Hogg. Eliza took the leadership, or rather, she took it back. Indeed, she was the one who had been in charge of Harriet since her childhood. She abandoned her to Shelley for the few weeks necessary for the wedding; however, she was now entering their home, just like the captain of a boat. Eliza raised her own flag up the mast, and from that moment, she would not tolerate any other master on board.

She even started to criticise Shelley's behaviour: "So, if I had not come, he was leaving you all alone with that young man… This is unconceivable! … For god's sake! What would Miss Warne say?... And this young man calling you 'darling Harriet'? Furthermore, you seem to tolerate it!"

When Hogg suggested a walk: "How dare you ask," said Eliza. "Harriet is tired, very unwell…."

"Harriet?" said Hogg, stunned. "What is happening to her? My god!"

"She is badly anxious; one has to be blind not to see it!"

And when Harriet wanted to read to Hogg the chaste precepts from Idomeneus he actually badly needed to hear: Eliza said "Reading aloud, Harriet? What about your anxiety? For god's sake! What would Miss Warne say?"

"Who is Miss Warne, for heaven's sake?" Hogg whispered to Harriet, taking advantage when the terrible Eliza retired to her bedroom.

"Miss Warne is Eliza's best friend… We rely a lot on her opinions."

"Why? Is she a remarkable person by birthright or education?"

"Miss Warne? O, no! She is the daughter of a café shop owner, just like us."

Hogg sighed and gazed up.

"And what is Eliza doing in her room? Is she reading?"

"No."

Harriet leaned towards him and said with a mysterious tone: "She is brushing her hair."

"Harriet, let's go!"

Harriet refused at first. However, since the hair brushing was taking time, finally, she agreed to go with Hogg for a few minutes.

Since his first attempt, Hogg had been trustworthy and respected his promise to be well behaved. This actually both reassured and disappointed Harriet. She was convinced of her virtuous power to resist; however, it was not displeasing for her to experience and struggle. On the bridge, Hogg stopped. With extreme speed, the swollen river swept along all sorts of whirling remnants.

"Darling Harriet, can you imagine Eliza here… she would whirl and whirl with her long black hair, just like that wooden beam… Oh, my god, what would Miss Warne say to that?"

Harriet turned away her face, then laughed out loud; Hogg could be quite sacrilegious. However, he was so funny, really.

"What a beautiful laugh you have, my dear Harriet. So joyful, so healthy!"

The valiant Harriet happily felt the beginning of another battle.

11
WHO WAS HOGG? (CONTINUED)

Earlier than expected, Shelley arrived the following day. He had not resolved anything. Mr Timothy still did not wish to see him. Indeed, he considered this marriage ceremony as a fundamental crime.

"I would have agreed," he said to Captain Pilfold, "to pay for the care of illegitimate children. But marriage? … Please. Do not talk to me about Shelley anymore."

Miss Hitchener, afraid of possible gossip, had refused to accompany Shelley; while going through London, he heard that Eliza had not waited for him; he so came back tired and melancholic, hoping to find rest around his spouse and his dear friend.

But from the moment he arrived, he felt an air of discomfort and constraint in this small society. Shut away in her room, Eliza brushed her long hair most of the day. Hogg and Harriet, rather than teasing one another around the teapot with bursts of laughter, were staying away from each other. And when Hogg addressed Harriet, she replied with a curt tone full of mystery.

"Dear Harriet, said Shelley as soon as they got together, "I do not like the snobbish tone you use with Hogg… he is my best friend; he has cared for you while I was away. To have your sister with you is not a reason to neglect a man, who I consider as a brother."

Harriet sighed. "What a nice friend," she said, with an air full of insinuation.

Surprised, Shelley requested further explanation. She said: "Twice he made declarations… the first time, he told me that he was crazy in love with me… I tried to laugh about it… I stopped him from speaking further… I thought it was over and was thinking of not telling you, not to worry you about it. However, yesterday, he talked again… he said that he could not live without me, that he would kill himself if I was not his."

Shelley felt that he was instantly freezing. A strange feeling of sudden death stopped his heart.

"Hogg? Hogg did this…but did not you tell him…?"

"O! I told him everything one can say… That his friendship was lacking… that it was untrustworthy to you…. 'Does this all matter when one loves?' he replied to me. 'It is Shelley who, cold and pure, should discourse about virtue, but as for me, I love you, the rest is nothing… Indeed, what wrong could we do to Shelley? He will never know. Why not promise me your love while you keep affectionate towards him? Does he look after you very much?'"

"Did he say that?"

WHO WAS HOGG? (CONTINUED)

"Yes, and more… he said you were mixing reasoning whenever and where it has nothing to do with. He said you are passionate and interested about chimera but icy about true feelings, which are the only things which count in life. To which I replied to the best I could."

Shelley let himself fall in the sofa. He felt that a grey veil was suddenly covering the whole world. His ideas swirled in a terrible moral dizziness. He shivered.

"Hogg tried to seduce my wife. He chose the moment I asked him to care for her, to protect her… this face I looked at with so much affection… I thought that if anyone could look at it, like I did, its air of loyalty would bring peace… When I was only loving such a villainous… Yet his attitude in Oxford was so righteous, so altruistic… I must talk to him; I must discuss it with him…"

He gave a long kiss to Harriet and asked Hogg to follow him out of the city. Hogg expected a dispute and was ready for it. He did not deny anything at all. On the contrary: "Yes, it is true… I loved Harriet from the first day I saw her in Edinburgh… Is that my fault? It is the way I am. I am transported by the beauty of women. Harriet is admirably beautiful… I repeat, I loved her at the first sight."

"This is not love, this is desire, a crude instinct. It is not that noble passion, which separates the human being from the beast, Love. Think, Hogg: love supposes the denial of the self together with the search for happiness of the loved one; you can only bring misfortune to Harriet… And so, your feeling is not love; on the contrary, it is selfishness…"

"Name it as you wish… Whatever the word, it is a terrible passion; I would have tried to resist, however, I felt it was invincible."

"No passion is invincible… the will can deal with any passion… If only you had thought about me… I have to admit that I suddenly feel older, more wilted by this news than by 20 years of misery… I feel my heart flaccid… And poor Harriet… Do you believe that the situation could not be painful to her?"

Hogg was drooping. He seemed ashamed and sad, and so he was. He loved Shelley, too, and judged himself harshly: "No woman," he thought, "is worth sacrificing such a friendship." So he said out loud: "I am sorry for what happened, Shelley; I will try to forget. I wish for your forgiveness and Harriet's, and then, we could start again our life together. Please stop being angry with me."

"I have no anger against you: I hate your mistake, not you. I hope that one day, you will look at your terrible outrage with as much disgust as me. That day, you will cease to be responsible for it. The man who repents is guilty no more. Furthermore, I shall not rebuke you."

Shelley was so pleased to have managed to control his anger and jealousy, and furthermore to have found the path of salvation for Hogg. Subsequently, he nearly forgot about the outrage.

However, women are far less forgiving. When Shelley came back and said that he had forgiven the culprit: "What!" Eliza said, "You wish to carry on living with this man? My goodness! But what will become of Harriet's poor nerves…" The next day, when Hogg came home from the law firm, he found the house empty.

12
FIRST ENCOUNTER WITH MATURITY

Fleeing from the deplorable Hogg, Shelley and the women decided to leave for the Lake District. Similarly to Poland Street, a sentimental reason attracted him to that region. Two great liberal poets, Southey and Coleridge, had been living there for quite a while, and serendipity may bring about a meeting between them all. Nothing more agreeable could happen to him than finally meeting the rare great men who were known to share his ideas.

At Keswick, they rented a small cottage, surrounded by flowers. Tenants did not have access to the garden, but the owner (who simply considered Shelley and Harriet as lost children) allowed them to enjoy it. Soon, the postman felt the weight of Shelley's post.

There was first the correspondence between him and Hogg, which was really discouraging. Hogg wrote Harriet long letters, where he swore to respect and love her for eternity. The persistence of his love made Harriet both tired and proud.

When Shelley said, "both distanciation and time will lead Hogg to forget," Harriet, dubious, shook her head. Even though, sincerely saddened by the wounds inflicted on her admirer, to hear that these wounds could not be deadly disappointed her: "Distance," she said, "calms down trifling passions, however it does increase great ones." When Hogg wrote: 'I shall obtain Harriet's forgiveness, otherwise I shall blow my brains out at her feet', even in sadness, she triumphed. Even though, she was reassured no gunshots happened to disturb their flowery solitude, she was somehow disappointed.

Then, there were letters from Miss Hitchener, Shelley's only confidant left, following Hogg's decadent behaviour. Nearly every day, several insistent and virtuous pages were sent. Harriet, herself, added to her husband's passionate discourse, offering warm invitations to come and join them.

The Duke of Norfolk was living close to them. He had once managed to reconcile Shelley and his father. Because money was once more becoming a pressing and major issue, Shelley and Harriet decided to write to him. His majesty responded amicably and invited Shelley, his wife and his sister-in-law to come to his castle over the weekend. He was interested to meet the rebellious young man, possibly because of natural goodwill or because of his duty as the head of a political party. The duke of Norfolk had indeed to ensure the good feelings of a young man destined to become, at legal age for adulthood, a Member of Parliament and inherit £6,000 annually.

At Greystoke Castle, Harriet shone. The duchess, who had been warned about the odd marriage of

Shelley, was agreeably surprised by his wife's elegance and culture. Even Eliza was not disagreeable to her. This particular visit had the best result possible; all danger of poverty was finally put aside. Hearing about his two daughters staying a few days at a duke's home, and that his son-in-law had been invited with one guinea in his pocket, Mr Westbrook felt transported by generosity. He agreed on the spot to send the couple an annual pension of £200. Mr Timothy could not appear meaner, especially when his overlord and master was asking him to be charitable. He resumed his son's £200 annuity.

In Shelley's mind, to have obtained this result without any concession on his part, was actually the most important fact: "I believe it is my duty," he wrote to his father, "to tell you that, whatever advantage I should gain from this, I just cannot promise to hide my opinions about religion and politics… such a way would be undignified for both you and me." To which Mr Timothy replied: "If I agreed to grant you a pension, it is only to prevent you swindling strangers." Mr Timothy was incapable of understanding any greatness of feeling.

* * *

At Greystoke Castle, Shelley met William Calvert, a friend of Southey who offered him to escort him to the poet's home. And so, for the first time, he would see in person a writer he admired.

Southey surprised Shelley who used to associate the idea of a poet with the most charming aerial objects. He found, in a rather comfortable and well heated house, Mrs Southey who looked more like a housewife than a muse. She used to be a seamstress and was binding her husband's books with pieces of cloth. Her linen cupboards were consecrated locations, where she exercised her ingenuity. She spoke about money, cooking and servants like a fishwife. The poet did not seem to notice such disgrace. He seemed to be a good, brave man. However, he did not think with appropriate reasoning. He admitted the fact that society needed to change. However, he added this would take a long time. He used the dreaded formula: "Neither I or you will ever see it"; he was hostile to Irish Catholic emancipation and to any radical measures. Worst of all, Southey said that he was Christian. Shelley left disappointed.

The good Southey was far from comprehending the impression he had made: "Strange young man," he thought after his visitor's departure… "to be the heir of a large domain seems to be his biggest sorrow. He is worried about his annuity of £6,000, when at his age, I was worried not to have a penny… Other than that, I think I am seeing my own ghost. He thinks he is an atheist when he is only a pantheist. This is a disease of youth that we all must go through. He has run into the right person; he could not have found a better doctor. I prescribed him Berkeley. He should become a follower before the end of the week… also, he was surprised to have met for the first time in his life a man who understood him… So, God help us! The world needs betterments, that is true. This young Sir Shelley does not seem to know how to work at it. However, I do not despair of convincing him that he can do a lot of good with his £6,000 a year."

And so, youth met maturity: youth was watching advancing age with an impatient respect, while maturity was contemplating youth with a benevolent irony and promised itself it could easily dominate with the power of a well-trained spirit. However, maturity was forgetting that spirits from successive generations are as disconnected as the monads of Mr Leibniz.

Southey and his wife did everything in their power to help the Shelleys. The poet, very popular in the county, went to see the owner of the cottage to obtain a reduction in the rent. Mrs Southey gave Harriet, still useless with housekeeping, very sound advice about cooking and laundry. She lent some bedsheets and tablecloths. This was from her a demonstration of goodwill. However, Shelley discovered something new that made his mature counterparts' advances devoid of sense.

Indeed, Shelley read in a review one of Southey's articles, where the old king of England was referred as "the best king ever to be enthroned". It was, of course, a slightly exaggerated adulation, Southey wanted to become the Poet Laureate. The way to such official honour has its challenges and codified means.

However, Shelley did not forbid such a mean attitude; he informed Southey that he considered him as a wage-earning slave, a supporter of crime, and would see him no more.

* * *

He forgot about Southey, when he found out that Godwin, the great Godwin, the author of *Political Justice*, the marriage destroyer, the enemy of the divine, the atheist, the republican, the revolutionary was alive. He was living in London. The great Godwin had a home address, and it was possible to write righteous letters to the prophet of virtue himself.

"You may be surprised," he wrote,

"To receive a letter from a stranger. No authorised introduction, and really none, will allow me what the common man would call this liberty; it is a freedom which is not regulated by society, yet is far from being unreasonable. The dearest interest for humanity requires that fashionable etiquette does not separate man from man.

The name Godwin has always inspired to me feelings of respect and admiration. I considered it as a light sparkling too brightly for the darkness around it… You should not be surprised by the inconceivable emotion triggered by the news of your very existence and of your actual home address. I erroneously added your name to the list of the illustrious dead; it is not so, you are alive, and I am convinced that you are still working on the happiness of the human race.

As for I, I have just entered the theatre of my work. However, my feelings, together with my reasoning, are what yours used to be. My short life has already been rather agitated… the bad treatment I have been submitted to has imprinted deep in my spirit the truth of your principles…"

When William Godwin received this letter, he found it instantly pleasurable. In fact, after being briefly celebrated following the publication of *Political Justice*, he had returned to relative anonymity. Like his romantic adept, he could also talk about his agitated life.

A clergyman during his youth, he then became at the age of 30 an atheist and a republican. In 1793, he published his famous book. Mr Pitt nearly pursued him at court. However, the high cost of the book, which was sold for 6 guineas, appeared to the minister a sufficient protection against the dangers of its theory. Four years later, Godwin married Mary Wollstonecraft, a genius wordsmith, who was already sharing his life. She sadly died during the birth of their daughter, and the enemy of marriage quickly married again with a widow, Mrs Clairmont, who lived next door and who had told him from her balcony: "Is it really possible that I am looking at the immortal Godwin?"

The life of this couple was difficult, though. He had five children from four different relationships: a daughter with Mary Wollstonecraft (a daughter of the genius by the genius and named Mary); two children from Mrs Clairmont's first marriage, Jane and Charles; one young boy, the son of Godwin and Mrs Clairmont; and finally, a young girl from the first marriage of Mary Wollstonecraft. This was the gentle and charming Fanny Imlay, Cinderella of Godwin's home.

The second Mrs Godwin was a rather vulgar woman wearing green spectacles, she demonstrated a bad temper and treated both Mary and Fanny very badly. To care for all these children, Godwin had started a publishing company of children books, while Mrs Godwin was looking after the bookshop. The life of the philosopher was difficult and sad, severely lacking the usual joy of vanity. A letter from a disciple in Keswick, and who wrote so elegantly, was so welcome. For a children book's publisher, overwhelmed by bills of exchange, nothing was more necessary and opportune than a man who addresses him as a luminary to dazzling for close inspection.

He replied that the letter did interest him, but that he would like to have more personal details. In return, he received a letter with a complete autobiography, where Mr Timothy and the head teacher of Oxford were mentioned with no great honour. He was also informed that Shelley was the heir of a £6,000 annuity, that he had married a woman with the same ideology, that he had published two novels and a pamphlet and that he would send these to his master if requested. Such a romantic letter was read with great interest by all the girls of the family Godwin-Clairmont. However, one point bothered the author of *Political Justice*. As the family's father, he recognised the value of paternal authority. He advised Shelley to be humble. It is possible that Mr Timothy Shelley had acted for his son's good. One should not be too judgmental, and certainly not publish one's own opinions. At his age, one should be a student. Why would he have the intolerable wish to become a master?

If anyone other than the venerable Godwin had written this letter, he would have been immediately considered as a paid champion of intolerance. However, youth always feel the need of so some kind of hierarchy and authority that. Even a rebellious young man happily adopts a master of conscience in front of whom he lowers himself with delight.

More than any other, Shelley's mystical soul needs to adore. "I only ask," he repeated, "to be a student; my humility and my confidence are both total when I am certain that no one looks to betray me and when I am with an indisputable and higher talent."

After having met Godwin, he became enthusiastic and started to plan greater projects. To transform and link together his destiny to other souls seemed easy to him. In the case of Harriet and Eliza, had he not succeeded? He decided that nothing could be easier than renting a mansion in Wales to gather Miss Hitchener and Godwin, his new 'venerable friend' with his charming family.

However, vexed by his master's scepticism, he wanted to prove with a dazzling example that despite his age, he could act. Before settling for life in this home of meditation, he would go with Harriet and Eliza to Ireland for several months. All three would work at hastening the emancipation of the Catholics, and in general a helping the condition of Ireland's poor people. How would Harriet and Eliza be able to emancipate the Catholics? This was never clearly explained. However, Shelley was bringing with him an already written 'Address to the Irish', so philosophical that one single reading of it would touch any heart.

And so, the young knight with sparkling eyes embarked to conquer the emerald isle. A manuscript replaced his spear, the young Harriet was his lady and the dark Eliza, as his squire, oversaw household money, housekeeping and all other trivial tasks.

13
SOAP BUBBLES

Le Chevalier de la Triste Figure ended up being pilloried by the prisoners he wanted to free. Shelley was greeted with hissing when, at a meeting of Catholics, he announced that it was wrong to deny Irish public functions as Catholics, because any religions deserve the same. His listeners preferred a hundred times more their persecutors' fanaticism than the scepticism of their helper.

The famous address had the same tone. It demonstrated that the emancipation of the Catholics should be the first move towards total freedom, Goodness, rather than skills, should be the principle for any politics, and that rather than waiting to be freed by the British, Irish people should liberate themselves by becoming just, charitable and temperate.

Shelley believed that his theory would reach the hearts of the poor people in Dublin. To preach this gospel, he was ready to become a martyr.

Harriet was no less enthusiastic and made the work of the reformer quite charming. The childish couple strolled Sackville Street with pockets full of leaflets. When they met a man or even a woman with a 'likely air', they gave papers for their redemption. From the balcony of their small apartment, they dropped the angelic theories on the passers-by. Once Shelley skilfully threw a pamphlet into the hood of an elderly woman, while Harriet ran away laughing. The conversion of the Irish became an amusing game.

Shelley's friends, Godwin and Miss Hitchener, were worried, expecting their arrest any day; the teacher even talked of political murder. However, Dublin Castle seemed to have acknowledged without too much concern that a young Englishman of 16 to 20 years had made a speech about morality. The police passed to the State Secretary one of the leaflets with his address. This document, where Shelley was asking his brothers for sobriety and charity, was judged quite stupid by the representatives of the king.

Such impunity was discouraging; the Irish way of life was even worse. "The reason why they drink a lot of whisky," said the good Harriet, "is because meat is too expensive." One day Shelley called for pity and tried to save some drunken man from being arrested for theft or brawling. The policeman, with a smile of pity, proved to him the man was drunk. On Saint Patrick's night, when all of Dublin is drunk dry, there was a ball at the castle. Percy and Harriet watched the starving people queuing around the State carriages to gaze at the finery. Such a want of dignity made Shelley despair.

To exemplify simplicity, the three started a vegetarian diet. Shelley liberated himself from any remorse about "the horrific slaughterhouses" or even about "the massacre of chickens". No one was spared the rule, apart when Mrs Nugent joined them for dinner. She was their only friend in Dublin, and a dressmaker. One of the difficulties of their mission was indeed the absence of relatives or friends among the Irish, who they dearly loved. "I suppose," Harriet said, "we shall know all of them once Percy becomes famous."

However, Percy became disheartened. In the land of unrealistic constructs where he spent most of his time, oppressed Ireland had resembled a beautiful feminine and proud entity, and Shelley was a knight and an apostle ready to fight and suffer for it; mobs of people dressed in rags were following him; barbaric British soldiers were arresting and whipping him. However, the heroical gentleness of his speech would be a charm for the oppressors themselves, and philosophy would become the miracle which reconciled the rival nations.

Slowly, this animated and sparkling image was disappearing. A last remnant of iridescent mist floated at the corners of the sombre black houses, then the true Ireland was there: an enormous and tangible mass of cities, farms and forests; an assembly of unfathomable and different human beings; secular piles of traditions, lores and laws; a land for playing, hunting, private revenges; the magistrate's chair, the soldier's garrisons, a territory for the police: Ireland miserable and derisive, suffering and talkative, unhappy and delighted to be upset; enigmatic island, absurd island… In face of this pressing reality, what could he do? What could he hope for? He was tired and overwhelmed by it.

Godwin, because of his growing power, supplicated his student to renounce this enterprise. Since Shelley had written that he considered him a father, Godwin took a grumpy and hostile tone. "Believe me, Shelley," he prophesied, "you are actually organising a bloodbath." If only he could have seen his son writing a harmless "proposal for an organisation for the good of humankind", while Eliza was sewing a red cap and Harriet was preparing a meal with honey and fruit, he would have been less concerned.

His demands were at least useful, because they became for Shelley the basis of an excuse to renounce becoming the champion of an oppressed people who were in all truth not interested in his cause. Apart from a few poor individuals who knew to find in him some help, no one in Dublin was taking him seriously. For an Irish person, an Englishman who loved Ireland was considered even more ridiculous than a regular Englishman. And if there is any spectacle a man who had studied in Eton and Oxford cannot stand being was the Irish disorder. Having seen the madness and the poverty of this nation, Shelley could not but think with intensity about the beauty and peace of the British countryside.

"I submit to you," he finally wrote to his "venerable friend", "I shall never again talk to illiterates… I shall only dedicate myself to a cause which shall remain effective long after I become a speck of dust."

Harriet packed all the remaining pamphlets and sent them to Miss Hitchener's address, who would have preferred to avoid such 'inflammable material'; Eliza folded her red coat. The three apostles took the boat.

*　*　*

Thereafter, the second phase of their programme was to rent a house in Wales to unite there "the spiritual team", with the purpose of resolving all dilemmas.

They thought they had found an acceptable shelter where Shelley, all alone, had escaped before his wedding. The charming wilderness of the countryside was attractive. Close to the house, he used to dangerously navigate a one-foot basket in the mountain stream. A £5 note was its sail, a terrified cat, its passenger. He was hoping Miss Hitchener's father would join them and care for the farm of the house.

However, nothing got resolved. The house was too expensive. Mr Hitchener was rather shocked by the gossip in Cuckfield about his daughter and Shelley. He forbade her to leave. The teacher, unconcerned and proud of the invitation, informed the whole village. People, and firstly Aunt Pilfold, drew conclusions without any goodwill. Shelley was again surprised by people's nastiness. He, who had kidnapped his wife for love, and married her in the customs of Scotland, could not be unfaithful to his Harriet! The very idea stunned him so much, that a woman less virtuous than the innocent Hitchener would have found it displeasing indeed.

As for the father, Mr Hitchener himself, he got treated as he deserved. He had been a café shop owner too, as the gods seemed to take pleasure in connecting the crystal-clear Shelley with members of this trade. "Sir," Shelley wrote to the father of his friend, "I find it somewhat difficult to avoid unwarranted surprise in reading that you are refusing my invitation to your daughter. Have you got the right to do so? Neither the laws of nature, nor the laws of England have ever put children at the level of private property… Goodbye! I hope that when I shall next hear from you, time will have made your feelings more liberal."

* * *

Since they had to leave Wales, Godwin pointed out a pretty cottage that one of his friends was renting out. Any advice from him inspired only respect; Shelley and Harriet travelled to the place but were disappointed. The house was quite plain, not fully finished and too small for them. However, on their way back from this futile journey, they discovered a bucolic village. Thirty thatched cottages covered in climbing roses and barberry shrubs composed the delightful village of Lynmouth. By a miracle, one of the cottages was available for rent. It happened to be the best placed one, towering beautifully above a wooded gorge. From the windows, one could glimpse at the sea, 300 feet below. On the spot, they decided to settle there for their whole life.

Once informed, the "venerable friend" wrote a quite sharp letter. He wrote that Shelley's tastes were too lavish, and that a small house, however humble, should have sufficed for what his student was talking about. If this letter had been written by Mr Timothy himself, Shelley would have objected more violently. However, it is natural to withstand from a stranger what cannot be from a father. Shelley thought not to blame him, but to write some justification and explanation. If he had said that the house recommended by his master was not good enough, it was not because of the idea of luxury or even of comfort. The number of rooms was simply insufficient. The consequent and logical necessity for two people of the opposite sex, not united by some kind of intimacy to sleep in the same room was in his view just inappropriate.

He knew that in an idyllic society, this principle or delicacy would cease to exist. However, at present, promiscuity appeared to him as dangerous. He exposed this idea with great caution as he feared it to be too reactionary. The master accepted to forget about it all.

The beautiful house in Lynmouth soon became the scene for an important event: the arrival of Miss Hitchener. Shelley trusted that she would bring with her an important element of intellectual collaboration, which he currently missed. Harriet was not losing anything really, because, in his mind, his spiritual sister would help to educate her. He thought they both had a strong enough mind to accept each other's rules.

The people of Lynmouth were surprised to see him romantically strolling along with a slim stranger though. It was with her that from that time he talked about plans he had to broadcast his ideas. The propaganda for virtue was becoming difficult though. One printer from London had just been condemned and punished at the pillory. Galileo's destiny did not scare Shelley himself. However, he could not endanger one innocent printer because of his own work.

Fortunately, the ingenious wordsmith had tricks at his disposal to defy Lord Castlereagh's police. When he had composed some incendiary pamphlets, sometimes he created a box coated with resin for the transport. And then, with a miniature mast and sail, he used to launch them in the ocean. Other times, he built hot gas balloons loaded with wisdom and launched them in the summer sky. And so, happy, he looked intensely at the sparkling small flames in the dark blue depths, or resin-coated boxes filled with a divine cure floating on the emerald waves.

After this magical work, his favourite pastime was to make soap bubbles. Sitting outside by the door, holding a pipe, he used to blow perfect and fragile spheres with the skills of a young girl. He watched intensely as the violet, green and gold hues sparkled within their elastic film, and then, changed and melted before fully disappearing.

Leaving for a short period the transparent and empty palace of logic, he felt a kind of obscure need to set one elusive beauty from a game of colours with rhythm and words.

14
THE VENERABLE FRIEND

Lynmouth's roses withered away; the autumn wind swept the clouds as if they were leaves; Miss Hitchener's prestige faded too. Harriet got tired of the perpetual presence of a stranger; even Shelley realised the disappearance of his ethereal vision, which had for long hidden some crude shapes. And, surprised to realise that he had in fact a mediocre and talkative woman by his side, first he tried in vain to find his past heroine but ended up regretting his foolishness.

After having insisted so hard to release her from school's duties, he found it difficult to get rid of her. Being with her in autumnal solitude became unbearable. In a big city, other friends or even theatre shows could have helped him forget this type of obsessive companion. In any case, Godwin called for Shelley to come back to London: he welcomed the suggestion and decided to leave, and for a longer period this time.

* * *

It was with emotion that one day in October 1812, they left their small hotel in St James Street to visit for the first time their friend Godwin and his family. Harriet, tiny, blonde with a pinkish face, trotted by the side of her tall and bent childish husband; they were both wondering what kind of welcome the philosopher's house would provide them. Miss Hitchener, while in London had visited Godwin, too, but was not made welcome. However, this did not prove anything, other than may be some perspicacity from Godwin.

They found the whole family gathered in the library of the Skinner Street house. The philosopher himself was there, a small and shabby man, bold, seemingly clever, looking like a methodist pastor, just like all the theorists of the French Revolution of the time. Mr Godwin's second wife was wearing a beautiful black silk dress and her green glasses, only for the time necessary to look properly at the grandson of a baronet and his beautiful wife. The Shelleys were informed that she was slanderous. However, that night, she seemed likable to them. Fanny Imlay, gentle and melancholic, was there too with Jane Clairmont, pretty with an Italian look, olive skin and a vivacious spirit.

"The only person missing is my daughter, Mary," Godwin said. "She is in Scotland. She looks very much like her mother, whose portrait I will now show you."

He invited the young couple round his library and Shelley looked intensely and with an emotional attraction at the portrait of the charming famous Mary Wollstonecraft. And then everyone sat down. Godwin and Percy talked at length about the connection between matter and spirit, the current situation of the clergy and about German literature. The women listened with awe. Harriet thought that Godwin looked alike Socrates, with the same bossy bold head and that Percy resembled one of the beautiful Greek disciples whose respect is tempered with impatient fervour.

* * *

A close intimacy built up between the Shelleys and the Godwins. Often,Godwin came to the hotel and invited Shelley for a walk, or Mrs Godwin invited Percy and Harriet for dinner; Eliza and Miss Hitchener, too, even though the latter somehow reluctantly. Harriet herself occasionally risked hosting a dinner.

One night, on 5th November, a day when firecrackers are ignited all over England in commemoration of the Gunpowder Treason plot, the Shelleys were dining at Godwin's. After dinner, young William, who was only 9, announced that he was going to join his neighbour, young Newton, to light some fireworks together. At that moment, Shelley was discussing an important matter with his venerable friend. The two words firecrackers and powder awoke the mind of the former alchemist from Field-Place. He hesitated a few seconds before leaving Godwin and the discussion. Visualising sparkles lighting up the old streets of London had won him over. He said to young William: "I shall come with you," and then he left.

Following the fireworks, young Newton, delighted to have an adult friend who played like a child and knew marvellous stories, brought him to meet his parents. Shelley accepted and did not regret. Indeed, he found the conversation with Mr and Mrs Newton just delightful. Immediately, a relaxed conversation, knowledgeable and agreeable, began. Mr Newton was made to please Shelley; he was a man obsessed by theories which he knew how to apply. His preferred idea was that humans, after migrating from the warm climate to the north where they had initially emerged, adopted an unnatural way of life, causing all subsequent misfortunes.

One of these bad habits was to put clothes on, and so Mr Newton made his children go naked at home. Another bad habit that humans acquired in migrating to the North was to eat meat. And so, the whole family became vegetarian. Nothing more could appeal to Shelley. Furthermore, Mr Newton added arguments that delighted him:

"Human beings do not resemble any carnivores; one does not have any claws to hold prey: one's teeth were made to eat fruit and vegetables. One gets sick as soon as one eats meat, which is actually poisonous for human beings. This is the meaning of Prometheus's fate, evidently a vegetarian myth. Prometheus, as a parable for humanity, created fire and cooking; then a vulture gnawed his liver. This vulture represents hepatitis, that is obvious!"

Indeed, ever since the family had adopted this new regime, none of them ever needed any drugs or even doctors; the children were the healthiest one could have met, and Shelley, who often met the little girls, all naked, found them perfect models for a sculpture.

He became a great regular in this house. As soon as his voice was heard, the five children jumped downstairs to meet and guided him to the nursery. He did not have any less success with their mother and her sister, Madame de Boinville.

At Godwin's, Fanny and Jane eagerly listened to him the whole evening. They admired his beauty. The strength of his logic seemed to them invincible. Even in a republican family, this young aristocrat, heir of a great wealth and so disdainful about money, had a romantic prestige indeed. And on his side, among the two young girls, Fanny kind and shy, Jane fierce and passionate, he recollected with a delicious mixture of sensuality and enthusiasm the beautiful evenings when his sisters and cousins had been around him, a long time ago.

Harriet was not quite as appreciated. Fanny and Jane quickly realised that she was not thinking much by herself, that she kept repeating her husband's favourite phrases and that her syntax was faulty.

"Poor Shelley," they all said when the couple had left. "He does not have the woman he deserves."

This is a feeling young girls develop easily towards a man they feel they ought to have in their life. Furthermore, they ventured to criticise the absent Harriet with barely perceptible remarks. Intuitively, they found out which one of them would irritate the dogmatic husband.

" I am intimidated by Harriet," kind Fanny wrote. "She is a handsome lady".

Shelley was in shock.

"How can Harriet be a handsome lady? You accuse her of this crime, the most unforgivable in my own eyes? The easiness and simplicity of her manners have always been greater than her greatest charms, and actually are not compatible with neither fashionable society, nor with any attempt to imitate its vulgar and shining glow. That is an opinion you cannot convert me to, as long as the live testimony of its error shall remain close to my eyes."

Thereafter, Fanny's letter will come back to Shelley's mind.

15
WHO WAS MISS HITCHENER?

After a year of exile in York, Hogg, fully reconciled with his family, went back to London to finish his law course.

One evening, dressed in a heavy dressing gown, peacefully reading in a comfortable armchair, a hot teapot on the table, he heard a violent knock at the front door. Then the door was flung open, making the walls tremble. The commotion evoked instantly sparkling eyes and a tall, bent body.

"If Shelley was still my friend," he thought… "only he…"

Then rapid steps on the stairs, those very light steps he had heard before in Oxford corridors.

"Never before, apart from Shelley, had anyone gone upstairs that way."

Then the door to his room opened and Shelley appeared, without any hat, open shirt, as always, wild, intellectual, similar to Ariel, the celestial spirit fallen down to Earth by mistake.

"I got your address from your employer… not without difficulty, though! He talked to me like I was a brigand and did not want to give it to me… How have you been over the past year? I've just come back from Ireland… I went to advise the

Irish Catholics about humanism… Thereafter, we went back to Wales, it was nice… Harriet is doing well… She is pregnant… Have you read Berkeley yet?... At the present time, I am reading Helvetius… It is clever, but dry…"

Hogg stared at him with the same affectionate and ironic admiration of the past: only Shelley could talk about Helvetius in the first sentence addressed to a friend he had not seen for a year, and especially following such serious disagreements. Shelley, agitated and joyful, was walking up and down the room, opened some books, asked questions but did not wait for answers, and really seemed to have totally forgotten that Hogg had in the past offended him.

He talked until late at night. Some of the neighbours banged the walls complaining about the clear, sharp voice that was preventing them from sleeping. Hogg, afraid about his reputation in the house, suggested Shelley to leave. However, Shelley kept talking. He started to explain that he needed to start a subscription to build an embankment to help to regain some land from the sea. He had himself subscribed for £100 and was dedicating his strength, his wealth, and his life to the project… Hogg then took him by his arm towards the door. However, Shelley kept resisting.

"Your neighbours are bothering us… these vile creatures do not know that the soul can only really feel free at night."

Hogg managed to bring him to the landing.

"I will leave, but on one condition: tomorrow night, you must come for dinner. Harriet shall be happy to see you again… I should first apologise for a horrible creature at home too: Miss Hitchener. However, she should leave within the next two days."

"Miss Hitchener, your soul's sister?

"Her?" Shelley said, "… a despicable, crawling worm! We now call her the brunette devil."

Once they both reached the door, Hogg freed himself gently and closed it behind him.

The following night, he presented himself at the hotel. Harriet received him with enthusiasm. She looked younger and even more radiant and charming than ever before.

"What a long separation it was!" she said. "However, this shall not happen ever again… we are coming to settle in London."

Eliza was sitting in a corner, haughty and quiet; she shook Hogg's hand without talking to him.

"Harriet, you look amazing, I must say," Hogg said.

"Her?" Eliza said with a languid voice… "Oh no! poor thing!"

"Nothing has changed," Hogg thought, "I should remain careful in this house."

At that moment, Shelley came in at the speed of light and dinner was served.

After the meal, Eliza whispered mysteriously to Harriet, who, obedient, went to say goodbye to Hogg and invited him to come back next Sunday morning.

"It should be the day of departure for the brunette devil. The conversation shall be difficult. As you are always gay, your presence should help us… Shelley talked to you about our tormentor, didn't he?

At the evocation of Miss Hitchener, Eliza demonstrated quiet disgust.

"She is a terrible woman," Harriet carried on. "She would have liked to be loved by Shelley; she even pretended that he did love her and that I was not good enough even to keep house. Percy is giving her a £100 annuity, with one condition, that she leaves."

Shelley confirmed the news. He understood the danger in giving up a quarter of his revenue. However, it was necessary: this woman had lost her status and, as she said, her reputation and her health were all ruined by their status as outcasts.

"She is indeed a horrible creature," he said while quivering… "Superficial, ugly, hermaphrodite… Sadly, I realised my initial misjudgement only after four months in her company. What could the hell be like, if such a woman was in heaven? And she is writing poetry! She has even written an elegiac for women's rights which starts like this: 'Everybody, everybody is a man. Women, like all the others…'"

He burst out laughing.

The next day, Hogg faithfully came; today's heroine seemed to him quite boring, yet harmless. She was a tall, bony and masculine woman, with dark skin tone and a thin beard. Soon Shelley announced that he had to leave; Harriet got a severe headache, which required isolation, and so Hogg ended up having to walk with the two Elizabeths.

With the brunette devil on his right arm and the black diamond, as he nicknamed Eliza, on his left arm, he walked towards St James's Park. "I could say, like Cornelia, 'These are my jewels,'" he thought. The two beautiful rivals fought over the head of the cynical man with calculated and snobbish phrases. The languid Eliza seemed awakened and dealt impressive strikes with a subtle pinch of malice. Miss Hitchener feigned to only talk to Hogg. She talked at length about women's rights. Eliza, who could shine only when theoretical subjects were discussed, found herself condemned by ignominy to silence. Back home, she stopped Hogg on the corridor corner:

"How have you been able to speak at length with this nasty woman? Why did you encourage her? Harriet will be very upset with you, very upset indeed."

However, Harriet, smiling simply said: "Are you not too tired of the brunette devil?"

After lunch, without any pretence, Hogg came back to the conversation about women's rights to provoke the Goddess Reason. Shelley left his chair to vehemently debate with her. The two Westbrook sisters looked at him with both horror and sadness, like he was guilty of consorting with the enemy.

Eliza went to Hogg and murmured in his ear:

"If you knew how dirty she is, you would not go so close to her."

And so when the time to prepare the exile's bags and boxes came, the women of Shelley's home rejoiced.

16
WHO WAS HARRIET REALLY?

The few months that followed Miss Hitchener's departure were a very happy time indeed. Although the Shelleys were still wandering and poor, their great intimate satisfaction created a kind of wealthy home around them. Shelley started a long poem, *Queen Mab*, and it became for him a sufficient purpose in his life. Harriet was pregnant, and a kind of pleasurable numbness helped him to focus all his energy on creativity. He stopped being bored when core intellectual work replaced inactivity.

During that time, they were living for short periods in Wales, at other times in Ireland, but not for a political purpose this time. To please Shelley, Harriet started to learn Latin. He was teaching his own way, without the grammar, leading her from the start to read Horace or Virgil. When she was studying, Shelley was working at his poem or reading history books. Godwin told him that his ignorance about history was the main reason for errors in his judgement, and, despite his dislike for the subject, he wanted to try. In the evenings Harriet sang Irish songs: *Robin Adair, Kate of Kearney*, or others. Or they read the newspapers, full of stories about court cases involving liberal writers. Shelley was writing to these individuals, unknown to him personally but convicted for their ideas, often to offer to pay their fine. Not having even £10 at his disposal, he had to borrow at 400 per cent the money he then distributed that way.

Soon, it became necessary to come back to London. Harriet's baby was due to be delivered soon, together with Shelley's 21st birthday, an important date for the relationship with his father and for possible negotiation.

They settled in a hotel, in a bedroom with a balcony above the street. Eliza, who was still with them, looked after Harriet with extra precautions which irritated Shelley, as he was himself an advocate for the natural way. When he was not there, Eliza started to educate her sister about matrimonial politics.

"It is most extraordinary, Eliza said, that at 21 years old, your husband cannot find a way to make up with his father, to make you welcomed by his family and to give you the life suitable for the wife of baronet-to-be. If you were more clever and more convincing, things would be different… you will soon have a child and this nomadic life shall become impossible. You must have your home in London, your own silver, your own carriage and everything, and it would be so if Shelley wanted it."

Harriet perceived and agreed with these arguments. She was beautiful and she knew it. A pretty wife does not tolerate well a life without luxury, just as a clever man cannot easily stand a subordinate state. The looks of passers-by told her about her own power. And she was aware that this power was actually ephemeral; just like a strong nation aims to find its place in the sun before demobilisation, the woman is aiming at dealing with the man, her enemy, before old age imposes on her full resignation. Indeed, Eliza felt sorry for Harriet.

Self-pity comes so naturally to all of us, that real and true happiness can easily be poisoned by the devious empathy of a stupid person.

Following Harriet's demands, whispered by Eliza but also by the renewed advice from the well-intentioned Duke of Norfolk, Shelley finally decided to have another try with his father. He would not have done so, if he did not feel that to try was both honourable and necessary. Also, he wanted so much to see his mother again.

After such a lengthy separation, Mr Timothy himself appeared to him harmless and rather pitiful. "My dear father, once again, I am taking the opportunity to try to establish again the relationship with you and the family, connections I lost because of my own madness… I hope that soon will be the moment we shall be able to look at each other, as father and son, with more trust than ever and that this will cease to cause trouble to the family's happiness. I was delighted to hear from John Grave, who had dinner with us yesterday, that you are in good health. My wife joins me in assuring you of our shared respectful feelings."

Sadly, Mr Timothy, incapable of silent triumph, requested from the repentant son the most impossible action. He requested that his son write to Oxford University's headmaster that he regretted the past incidents and that he had become a respectful son of the Anglican church. Otherwise, he could not communicate further.

"I am not so deprived of dignity," Shelley replied. "I cannot deny the ideas I trust as true. Any man with common sense needs to know that the denial of his serious convictions by simple order would show a lack of integrity. I would accept anything reasonable, that is, anything not affecting the loss of self-esteem, for life without it becomes a shameful hardship."

Eliza regarded such obstinacy as senseless: "So, Harriet, so close to giving birth, will not even have a carriage to avoid rushing through London on foot." Shelley, conceding, finally bought a carriage, but refused to ever use it himself. He hated being enclosed and driven; rather, he kept finding enchanting long walks through London with his friend, Hogg.

Indeed, if he was now tired of Eliza, he did not lack homes from friends to take refuge in. There was Godwin's, in Skinner Street, where Fanny and Jane Clairmont always welcomed him with such flattering enthusiasm. There was the Newtons' home, where he found clever affection together with refined and gentle manners. Furthermore, Mrs Newton played the piano beautifully. Shelley, sitting down on the carpet with the beautiful children, used to tell them stories of ghosts and spectres. Often, Madame de Boinville stayed at her sister's home. These two ladies, the daughters of a plantation owner in St Vincent, had a mix of French and English culture greatly appreciated by Shelley, who was a great admirer of the French philosophers. He found Madame de Boinville particularly charming. Her romance with a bankrupt emigrant, a friend of André Chénier and Lafayette, gave her a kind of poetic prestige. She was a woman with white hair and yet a childish face, with a wit so vivid and modern, that one found her more pleasurable to talk to rather to a young lady. In both, Shelley found for the first time female wits worthy of his. Eliza Westbrook and Miss Hitchener then seemed to him rather contemptible.

As the result of his life with Harriet, he had become used to considering women as childish; he thought that ideas, to be presented, had to be first depleted and simplified. However, in the presence of Madame de Boinville, he was surprised not only by the fact that he was able to go through his whole idea to the end, but also, by her elegant, precise use of language, she gave ideas a new attraction. For her and for her sister, ideas were, just like for him, the most beautiful and natural diversion. Culture is nothing without manners, and the mixture of the two in a woman is actually the most exquisite product of civilisation. From a secret joy and a delightful feeling of perfection, Shelley found himself in an environment that favoured his own happiness and realised that what he had known before was much inferior.

For these women too, the discovery of Shelley was rather intoxicating. This young, beautiful man from high society had a taste for ideas that he was able to develop with incredible energy. By that time, he had lost his teenage, rather authoritative, snobbism and demonstrated a humble grace while talking. They had never seen before a man without any sign of selfishness, a man so generous, so free from the material world. He demonstrated a confident ease, a denial of any ceremony, and at the same time the perfect politeness which makes young British aristocrats so charming. Indeed, what can be more charming than a saint who is a gentleman?

With a hint of jealousy, but also with a friendly curiosity, Hogg noticed the clever manoeuvres of so many beautiful women around his candid friend. In Godwin's home, the young girls called him the king of the elves or the fairies; in Newton's home, he was Oberon. As soon as he entered, the women gathered around him. However, it was not easy to call this spirit at a precise time. The king of the elves had strange demands, sudden fears, mad terrors. Sometimes, a poetic vision retained him precisely at the time when tea was about to be served; at other times, and precisely when one thought of him as rapt and submissive, an imaginary duty would pop up and he would leave on the spot for an unknown mission.

"There are countries," Hogg told him, "Where people believe that goats are diabolical animals and pass 12 out of 24 hours in hell. I believe that you are like the goats, Shelley."

On the other hand, when a woman according to her heart, was able to interest him and let him talk animatedly about the serious topics he loved, he just forgot the time and even where he was.

The night waned and Shelley would keep talking with ardour, like a beautiful Adonis surrounded by slightly panting priestesses. When dawn broke, he was still talking, and so, since it was too late to go to bed, a walk in the delicious dew gently ended the night's discussion.

"But, what on earth are you talking about around all these beauties all night?" Hogg, perplexed, specifically asked.

"I do not know."

Harriet also wondered about what her husband was telling these girls. In fact, she was approaching delivery and stayed at home most of the time. Quite often, Shelley left her alone. She did not feel welcome in the houses where her husband was adored. Once, at Godwin's home, she had an argument with Mrs Godwin. At the de Boinvilles, she had been welcomed as the charming wife of the poet, but then found to be rather mediocre.

17
COMPARISONS

The baby was a girl, a little blonde girl with blue eyes. His father named her Ianthe, to which the name Elisabeth was added by her mother; and so, one can say Ovid and Miss Westbrook met at her cradle. Shelley got into the habit of humming while walking with her in his arms. The idea of raising a child, a new being, and being able to save her childhood from prejudice were both appealing to him indeed. An admirer of Rousseau, he presumed that Harriet would nurse the child herself, and so he imagined the future, caring for these two beautiful creatures in all simplicity and with tenderness.

The odious Eliza was fully erased from the exaltation produced by this new rule.

However, Harriet, influenced by her sister, refused to breastfeed their daughter. She in fact employed a woman to care for her, a "mercenary", according to Shelley. She was quietly stubborn and remained invincible on the subject.

Since the child's birth, a strange metamorphosis had come over her. It seemed that Harriet wanted revenge after the lengthy inactivity imposed on her by the pregnancy. She did not resume her Latin lessons, which she had stopped during her three weeks in bed. Rather, she wanted nothing now but to be outside, looking in the windows of bonnet-shops and jewellers.

Getting pleasure from such activity was incomprehensible and scandalous for Shelley. He had agreed to pay for any of his wife's reasonable caprices, even at the cost of a loan. But wasting money much needed by some persecuted writer or rightful cause by spending money on rags and hats seemed to him just shameful.

He expressed his view sternly.

Eliza pointed out the obvious. "Your husband finds money to pay Godwin's debts: the man who tricks him and whose wife denies us any welcome; he found money to pay the fines of scribblers, but not to clothe and cover the head of his own wife. If he finds it inappropriate that a young and pretty woman wishes to please, he is just stupid and a Quaker. If you cannot shine with fine clothing at 18 years old, when will you be able to?"

Eliza eagerly invited to their home an officer, Major Ryan, whom they had previously met in Ireland. The major agreed that such a delightful woman as Harriet should live a life in accord with her true tastes. Harriet was ready to believe him. She recalled that Latin and philosophy were actually difficult for her to study. She did it without complaining because she loved and admired her husband.

However, in all due respect, she was mostly interested in shopping and gossip. It was like the revelation Shelley had experienced at the Newtons' home. The spontaneous and vivid pleasure she found contrasted with the painful concentration she previously applied to her husband's lessons.

Shelley thought that their stay in London was the cause of the problem; he had the idea (one of those lovers get spontaneously when feeling the coming of trouble) to leave and go back to the place where their love had been at its best.

Harriet's carriage was prepared. Shelley borrowed £500 and signed a bond of £2,000 on his inheritance, and together with Eliza, they left for a 'pilgrimage' to Keswick and Edinburgh.

The business of travelling helped them to forget their troubles; however, as soon as they arrived home, the disagreements came back just as much; Harriet and Eliza requested a pretty apartment, elegant living, a proper bathroom and a flattering social life. Shelley scorned such things and even more that his wife wanted them. Occasionally, fleeting moments of contempt passed across his still ardent love.

Hogg came to visit. He found Harriet fully recovered from the birth, prettier and rosier than ever before. However, she no longer offered to read him the wise counsels of Idomeneus; rather, she suggested he came with her to the trendy fashion boutique of the moment. There, she disappeared, leaving Hogg outside. He found her quite boring really. Because any man has limited forbearance for a woman who once rejected him. He told Shelley, who himself found it difficult to hide his feelings. The couple was reaching a dangerous stage now a third party had been confided in.

* * *

When Madame de Boinville invited both Shelley and Hogg to pass a few days in the countryside, they accepted with pleasure. They met her daughter, Cornelia, who was cultured, sad and pretty, and her sister, Mrs Newton. Shelley welcomed back the delightful impressions of previous soirees. He used to call Madame de Boinville 'Maimouna', because, like the heroine of his preferred poem, *Thalaba*:

> "…her face was as a damsel's face
> And yet her hair was grey."

The beautiful Cornelia taught them some Italian, while, with a pure voice, Madame de Boinville talked about the refined and compassionate theories of the French philosophers:

> *"To enjoy and give joy without ever hurting anyone,
> that is the whole morality"*

These words from Nicolas Chamfort and favoured by Madame De Boinville should have shaken Shelley. Poor Harriet herself had never said anything so much against virtue itself. However, she would not have been able to say it so nicely.

In Bracknell, even small talk was agreeable to Shelley, because any play on words seemed impregnated with deep thinking. Every morning, Cornelia used to read and even learn by heart one of Francis Petrarch's sonnets.

And then, she would meditate all day long about it. On their arrival, Hogg and Shelley would ask her first about the sonnet of the day. Sometimes, the poem was too moving for her to read out loud; and so, she would open the little pocket Petrarch she always had with her and point out the page to them.

And then, while walking along the path between the two young men, she talked about the love poem in question with both eloquence and simplicity.

"It is nice," she told them, "To start the day in that manner, I mean with some tenderness and kind feelings. This can perfume one's actions until the evening."

These walks and talks were about subjects which Shelley found true and important. This home, luxurious but simple, had a perfection which enchanted him. Everything about Bracknell was perceived by Shelley as a peaceful and relaxing environment.

Harriet was invited too; Madame de Boinville welcomed her with both kindness and snobbery. "She is indeed a very pretty young woman," she said to Hogg. "She seems slightly frivolous for our dear and exquisite Stoic, but she is only 18, is she not?"

Harriet felt that she was not treated as equal; she realised that Shelley enjoyed more reading Francis Petrarch with Cornelia than talking to her about how to increase the young family's daily expenses.

As a reaction against the new environment, despite the mask of goodwill, she became hostile, mocking and rather cynical. In moments full of solemnity, like when the group focused on the issue of the end of slavery or even about justice as a philosophical subject, Shelley spotted Harriet exchanging smirks with Hogg, or with Peacock, a new friend they had met recently.

While he could forgive Hogg's mockery, his wife's attitude irritated him very much. Hogg's mind was like a separate universe from his, a mind he accepted as different. However, Harriet's mind was in some way his own endeavour; he had trained her, raised and educated her; he had got used to seeing her as an echo. On suddenly realising that this very being, this other self, was now detached from him, and sometimes even smirked while listening to him, he felt a profound sadness.

Nothing renders somebody more stupid than unconfessed jealousy. Instead of confronting their rival directly, which might seem natural and even understandable, one instead mocks their most trivial actions, rarely using harsh words, but clumsily turning what might have been a genuine and justified feeling into something that appears quite petty. As a result, Harriet found everything bad in Bracknell because she was jealous of Cornelia.

Because of her pride, Harriet's attitude immediately worsened. "Eliza is right," she thought, "he is selfish and thinks that he is admirable… Because he loves this secluded life, his useless discussions and these Indian poems, he would like to impose all of this on me… however, how dare he forbid me my personal tastes? How can the life of a Cornelia reading Petrarch be more commendable than mine?... these women he admires are older and less pretty than me… He would soon miss me…"

She announced her plan to leave for London to be with Eliza. No one tried to retain her more than politeness required. "Poor Shelley," the Boinville ladies thought (like before them, the Godwin demoiselles), "poor Shelley, he does not have the wife he deserves."

Harriet then got into the habit of leaving him in Bracknell to stay with Eliza in London for longer periods. And soon, some 'kind' friends told Shelley that actually she was on occasion spotted walking by the side of Major Ryan.

For the first time since their wedding, the idea of unfaithfulness appeared to him as a possible concern in their life together. It was a consideration he had so far neglected and left in the abstract world of ideas. Suddenly, thinking of Harriet and himself both involved as characters in such a situation, he felt the most violent pain he had ever known.

With logic, he thought that he should be happy to have got rid of a mean and mediocre woman. If he was then feeling love, was it not for the delightful Cornelia Turner, rather than for Harriet, whose embittered vulgarity upset him so much at Bracknell? And if he did not love her anymore, was this breakdown not the easiest solution? Did he not teach everyone that the day love vanishes, both spouses should be allowed to get back their freedom? However, he reasoned and manipulated such truth in vain. Stupefied, he discovered the reality, which was that Harriet Westbrook and Percy Shelley were not anymore isolated and free individuals. Shared memories, caresses and suffering had enveloped them in an invisible yet carnal web, which painfully thwarted their shared desire to escape.

In a hurry, he went back to London, having decided to apologise, and even to plead guilty. However, he found Harriet tense, with a harsh, even ironical attitude, which made any in depth dialogue impossible. Such a change was beyond comprehension.

This child, so gentle, so submissive only three months before, was now haughty with a cold heart. In fleeting moments, Shelley thought he spotted fleeting glimpses of the Harriet he used to know, but when he then tried tender and loving words, he found only a freezing armour.

Without any aim, he wandered the streets of London: "How mad I have been," he thought… "I united for ever with a woman who does not love me, who had never loved me really… It is now clear to me that she married me only for my wealth and my title… She now considers her hopes as deceit and makes me pay for her frustration…" and then, repelled, he repeated himself: "A heart just like an ice pick, just like an ice pick."

It is possible that if he had been alone with her, he could have succeeded in getting back with her. However, Eliza was between them, hostile, tight-lipped and formidable, while the handsome major Ryan was in the background, ready to sympathise about the injustices of the wrongs of a dogmatic husband.

Following a few days of struggle, Shelley's ardour weakened suddenly. He was capable of extraordinary vitality, when nothing seemed impossible to him. But, like previously in Oxford after his walks, he now fell down in an irresistible torpor, his usual nervous drive like a dying flame which often sparkles prodigiously just before it totally expires.

When he realised that Harriet remained indifferent, he abandoned any hope of saving what remained of their union and went to Bracknell for a month-long holiday without her. He was aware, without any doubt, that after such a long absence, he would find her completely spoiled by her surroundings. He knew that following a charming break in Bracknell, a catastrophe would follow. However, he felt exhausted and could not carry on with the struggle.

"I have become," he said, "an insect warming itself while playing in a sun ray; and the next cloud would push me on and on towards hell and cold." Then, he recited methodically Burns' verse:

> *"But pleasures are like poppies spread,*
> *You seize the flower, its bloom is shed;*
> *Or like the snowfall in the river,*
> *A moment white, then melts for ever"*

In the crystalline structure of his mind, it seemed to him that Harriet, his daughter and Eliza were all falling apart, just like blocks of rebellious living matter. In vain, with all the power of logic, he tried to help them to escape.

18
SECOND EMBODIMENT OF THE GODDESS

There were days when Shelley, thinking about the pretty young face of his 18-year-old wife, believed that things could be forgotten and restored. In one melancholic poem, he tried to tell her how difficult it was for him to see only her freezing contempt in place of the warm sun in her eyes he used to contemplate. Was she touched by it? He would never know; she was enclosing herself deeper in hostility and secrecy. He left her alone more frequently; as probable revenge, when he got back to London, she left for Bath with her daughter.

Shelley had to remain in the city. Although he had reached the age of majority, his financial situation was still not set up adequately. His lawyer told him about the possibility of a court case requested by his family to withhold his rights. However, despite already being seriously in debt, he was obsessed with helping others in the same situation. The children's book publishing company set up by Godwin was approaching bankruptcy, and seeing this old fighter for rights diminished and sad because of his financial difficulties was just too harsh for the disciple. Three thousand pounds was required, a considerable sum indeed.

Because of his need for help, Godwin renewed his friendship with Shelley, and since he was now living like a bachelor, he invited Shelley to dine with them in Skinner Street, supposing that his beautiful other half was away on holiday for an indeterminate time.

Shelley accepted with great pleasure, knowing that he would see the young girls again; Godwin informed him that this time he would meet Mary, who was back from Scotland. He described her beautifully: 17, a vivacious wit, a great thirst for knowledge, an invincible perseverance. Fanny and Jane had already described her as clever as she was beautiful; her mother, Mary Wollstonecraft, had inspired great admiration in Shelley. He felt emotional knowing that he was about to meet this still unknown being.

To be happy, he needed to incarnate in a beautiful face the enigmatic and good forces that he believed were disseminated in the whole universe; love was for him passionate admiration, a complete act of faith, an exquisite and perfect mixture of sensuality and intelligence.

If Mary had not come, or if she had disappointed him, it is likely that this feeling flying around poor Shelley would have fallen on Fanny, or even on Jane. However, it was Mary he was waiting for.

Her face was pure and pale with fine traits, her blonde hair smoothed in a head band, forehead high, hazel eyes, serious and gentle. Her air of patient intelligence, courage and pride inspired immediately the same enthusiasm in Shelley as his previous reading of Homer and Plutarch. He could see something heroic in this delicate child. The mixture of heroic and feminine delighted him the most.

"How much seriousness and how much sensibility!" he thought, while listening with delight to her young voice. "A girl, beautiful and thoughtful, at the delightful age when the grace of a woman can be united with the intellectual curiosity of an ephebe." This had always been in his view, like a most exquisite work of art. As a result, he longed to embrace these delicate, fragile shoulders like a brother and to make those eager eyes shine with the thrill of an astonishing journey into the realms of abstract thought.

Harriet had only partially allowed this ideal to become reality. Briefly, he had hoped to find in her the charming mixture of beauty and intelligence that he could have so much loved. However, Harriet had failed the test of time. She lacked seriousness; even though she tried to be interested in ideas, her indifference revealed itself in the emptiness of her eyes. And certainly, she was coquettish, frivolous, and clever with women's ploys, and this was enough to make Shelley freeze.

On the other hand, Mary, with her hazel eyes, was as sharp as a blade. Raised by the author of *Political Justice*, her mind seemed free from any female superstition and her clear, high-pitched voice revealed delightfully its elegant precision. Every evening, in the small house on Skinner Street, Shelley dined, contemplating Mary at length. He seemed to listen carefully as Godwin discussed his dreadful state of affairs, England's finances or even the laws governing the media. However, his eyes often wandered.

Mary was ready to love him, too. The romantic preparation had already been done by her sisters, who had been writing to her over the past month about the beautiful poet. Their descriptions of Shelley did not do justice to the reality.

In an instant, she saw his interest in her. Even though he never complained, she saw that he was not a happy man. One evening, as they were together on their own in the room where Mary Wollstonecraft's portrait hung, she started to talk about her own issues. She adored her father; however, she hated Mrs Godwin. Because of her, the house in Skinner Street had become horrendous. The only place in the world where she felt safe was her mother's tomb. It was there that she meditated daily and read. Shelley, very much moved by what he heard, asked if he could join her one day.

And so, after five years, once again, he found himself in a cemetery, sitting close to a serious and passionate virgin. This time, the divine had morphed into a woman.

However, and sadly, Shelley was not a free man anymore. He felt attracted to Mary by some irresistible power. He desired holding this hand, kiss this mouth with a perfect arc; he felt that she desired him too, and so their eyes had to turn away from each other. However, what could he offer? He was a married man. Marriage was only a convention though, and, without any love left, he could consider himself as free. He never promised anything else to Harriet; furthermore, he believed that she was already Major Ryan's mistress. He no longer had any scruples about her. But his marriage being legally unbreakable, what could he give Mary? Could he tolerate her living as an outcast, when he could not accept it for his first love?

A love that is shared, even without hope, is worth more than uncertainty deepened by moral solitude. He decided to tell Mary the truth about his marriage.

Marital love, even when dying, behind an armour of silence, does endure longer than one thinks against the blows of life. However, there comes a time when a man finds a tender joy in expressing his pain. Shelley described Harriet as he saw her now, and unconsciously transposed some spiritual meaning to his deceit. He needed a companion who felt poetry and understood philosophy; Harriet could do neither. He found an aching pleasure in disapproving what he had lost.

He gave Mary a copy of *Queen Mab*. Under the printed dedication of the poem to Harriet, the muse of his songs, he had written: "Count Slobendorf was about to marry a woman who, only attracted by his wealth, proved her selfishness in abandoning him to jail." Mary, back in her room, added: "This book is sacred, no other creature apart me shall open it, for I should write in it whatever I wish. However, what will I write? That I love the author above every word which could be expressed but that everything is separating us, my dearest and only love. From that love that we promise to each other, I wish to be yours. I cannot be with someone else, I am yours, only yours…

> *"By the kiss of love, the glance none saw beside,*
> *The smile none else might understand,*
> *The whispered thought of hearts allied,*
> *The pressure of the thrilling hand.*
> *I have pledged myself to thee and sacred is the gift"*

"The look that no one else can see, the smile that no one can understand": Godwin had nonetheless seen and understood. Of course, his daughter's scheme with a married man was of concern to him. He tried to show the danger and asked her to stop seeing Shelley. He wrote to Shelley in the same way, advising him to reconcile with his wife and asked him to stop coming to Skinner Street until the passion had calmed down.

This ban, even if decided with good intention, promoted events which without it could have been at least delayed. Shelley, passionately in love with someone else, decided to leave his wife. In fact, he did not have any remorse whatsoever for Harriet, whom he considered the guilty one, despite Peacock and Hogg's statements as impartial witnesses. "She is only interested by one subject" he thought, "money… I shall care for her on that point and so she should be happy to get back her freedom." He asked Harriet to come to London with the view of letting her know about his plan. When she arrived in London, she was 4 months pregnant and quite unwell. When her husband told her, calmly and kindly, that he had decided to live without her and to flee with another woman, but would remain her most loyal friend, she became very sick indeed.

Shelley cared for her with a dedication which made things even worse. However, as soon as she got better, he resumed his inflexible line of reasoning: "The union between a man and a woman is sacred only if it contributes to the happiness of the two spouses, and so, it can break down as soon as the drawbacks win over the benefits. Loyalty is not virtuous in itself; it even contributes to vice, considering it tolerates wrongdoing, sometimes significantly, in its choice…

When he extended his transparent and insurmountable connected ideas around her, Harriet simply felt at loss. As before, when she had tried to defend her religious beliefs, she felt overwhelmed. She knew that one answer existed. The immense pain, the anxiety, the mixture of love and horror, all of this was needed to be expressed and that she could have found the answer if only her mind had been clearer. However, she just could not find out what she had to argue with to defend herself. Harriet imagined she was fighting against multiple invisible fortifications.

For relief, she let herself go with terrible rages against Mary. It was Mary who had cooked it all up; it was she who had managed to separate Shelley from his wife, speculated on his love for the romantic in inviting him for a date in a cemetery, an idea so attractive to Shelley's personality. In Harriet's eyes, Mary played outrageously on the memory of her mother too.

On her side, Mary thought about Harriet without any pity of any kind. She created an obnoxious image of her. She thought that a woman who, despite being fortunate to be Shelley's wife, had not been able to give him happiness, could only be selfish, useless and mediocre. She knew, though, that Shelley would treat his wife generously, that he was preparing a donation in her favour, and that he had ordered his banker to pay Harriet most of his own pension. This reassured her conscience. "She will get money, so she will be happy," she said scornfully.

Shelley was nervous and agitated. A kind of sentimental turmoil raged in him, with contradictory feelings fighting each other. When he saw Harriet falling into heartbreaking despair, he could not help remembering the not-too-distant past that had been enchanting. To get a few hours of calm, he used Laudanum, with, inevitably, a rapid use of stronger doses. He showed the bottle to his friend Peacock and said to him: "I am never parted from this." He added: "And I try to repeat to myself this verse of Sophocles you translated:

> *Man's happiest lot is not to be*
> *And when we tread life's thorny steep,*
> *Most blest are they who earliest free*
> *Descend to death's eternal sleep."*

PART TWO

Ariel: Was't well done
Prospero: Bravely, my diligence. Thou shalt be free

William Shakespeare

19
A SIX WEEKS' TOUR

A coach was ordered for four in the morning. Shelley waited all night on the pavement, just opposite Godwin's house. Finally, the stars and the lights grew pale. Mary, dressed for travelling, quietly opened the door. Jane Clairmont who, at the last minute, had decided to leave with her sister, busied herself whispering about their luggage.

Mary found the travelling quite long and tiring. Shelley was concerned about stopping in case Godwin was already on his way, pursuing them. Finally, around four, they arrived in Dover, where, following difficult negotiations with the customs officers and mariners, they finally found a small boat on which the seafarer agreed to take them to Calais.

The evening was just beautiful: as the great white cliffs slowly got smaller, the runaways felt finally safer.

However, the breeze started to blow to become soon a violent wind. Mary, feeling sick, spent the night lying across Shelley's knees. He was also exhausted, and tried his best to support her. The moon descended slowly towards the horizon. Then, in total darkness, a thunderstorm erupted, with lightning flashing over the dark, swelling sea. Finally, the daylight appeared, the storm went away, the wind weakened, and a large sun set on France.

In Calais' streets, Mary's torpor disappeared in face of the gay agitation of the harbour, the foreign language, and the picturesque costumes of the fishermen and of the women. While waiting for their luggage to be transported by Dover's mail steamer, they stayed all day at the inn. Mrs Godwin, wearing her green glasses, arrived with the steamer. The large woman was hoping to bring back Jane; however, Shelley's eloquence was more powerful, and Mrs Godwin went back alone. At six in the evening, the travellers left Calais for Boulogne with a carriage led by three horses.

* * *

The plan was to reach Switzerland. However, already in Paris, they had no money left. They had a letter of recommendation for a French businessman, Tavernier, who was supposed to find some money for them. They invited him for breakfast at the hotel and found him a perfect idiot, since he seems not to comprehend the absolute necessity of the journey of two young girls and one excited, tall, young man.

Shelley left his watch and chain as a pledge of repayment; in exchange, he obtained eight Napoleon coins. This was enough to eat for two weeks, and so, with a relaxed spirit, they started to explore the boulevards, the Louvre and Notre-Dame. But soon, they preferred staying at the hotel to read the work of Mary Wollstonecraft and Byron's poetry.

After one week, Tavernier, who was a good man, agreed to lend them 1,200 francs. It was not enough for the journey and the carriage, though. Therefore, they decided to leave by foot, and to buy a donkey for Mary. Shelley went to the animal market and came back to the hotel with a tiny ass; the following day, with his wife and his sister-in-law, the ass trotting behind, Shelley took a carriage to the gate of Charenton.

In 1814, French roads were unsafe. The army had been dismantled; gangs of marauding soldiers frequently mugged travellers. The workers in the fields gazed with an air of surprise at the caravan with two beautiful young girls in black silk dresses in the sole company of a teenager with curly hair and a donkey so ridiculously small.

After a few kilometres, the donkey got so exhausted that Shelley and Jane resorted to carry it. Arriving at a village, they finally sold the poor donkey and replaced it with a stronger mule and stayed there for the night.

The war had devastated the land; the villages were partly destroyed, the houses often had no roof, their beams blackened by the fire. When one asked a farmer for milk, he would reply cursing the Cossacks who stole his cows.

In the run-down inn, the beds were so dirty that Mary and Jane were afraid to go to sleep; big rats grazed them in the darkness. They got used to falling asleep sitting in the farms' kitchen. The large stove weighed down the atmosphere; the cries of the children, the crackles of the old wood, all got mixed up in the hazy daydreaming of half-sleep; Mary was worried and started to wonder if her father was suffering because of her flight; and Shelley was concerned about Harriet's isolation.

From Troyes, he wrote a long letter asking her to come and join them in Switzerland. She would live close to them, and she could count on being with a friend without selfishness. Quite naturally, he gave her news about Mary. This honesty appeared quite natural to him. He had no doubt that he could expect soon his wife's arrival. It is likely that one would judge this communal life quite licentious though; however, why should he care about others? Rather, should he not obey his feeling of pity, respond with tenderness rather than to their prejudices, which had no rational basis?

Harriet never replied.

From Pontarlier to Neufchâtel, they reach Lake Lucerne. Shelley wanted to settle in Brunnen, near the chapel of the famous Guillaume Tell, the defender of freedom. They rented two rooms for six months in the only free building of the area, a dilapidated old castle. They then bought beds, chairs, wardrobes and a woodburner. The priest and the doctor of the village came to visit them; Shelley started on the same day a novel,

The Assassins, with, in his mind, the reassuring possibility of settling here for good.

However, the wood-burner did not work and this despite Shelley's attempts. The bedroom became icy cold and full of smoke, while outside, the rain was beating on the windows. The three exiled young people found themselves very lonely indeed. And then, they remembered and started to talk together about English homes, so comfortable and cosy, about English tea, often hot and aromatic, or about the English sky, most of the time misty but gentle, and finally about English folk: cold but well intentioned, who spoke the same language, and could pronounce properly their names; of the British moneylenders, harsh but still helpful. Shelley counted what they had; they had only £28 left. A powerful desire animated all three. It was then that Shelley made and expressed the decision to go back.

As soon as the decision was made, they all felt happier. "It is amusing," Jane said, "that after only two days, we are leaving the rooms we have furnished and rented for six months with our own money. When I saw Dover's cliffs draw away, I thought that I may never see them again, and now…" These words were pronounced in the middle of the night. The next day, under a heavy rain, they took a boat to Lucerne, while in Brunnen, the priest was astounded to hear about their early departure.

From Lucerne, by ferry, they went to Bale and then to Cologne. The weather was pleasant. In the evening, under the stars, the mariners were singing some romantic ballads. Shelley was working on *The Assassins*; Mary and Jane, on their side, had both started a novel: the hills crowned with ruins inspired their romantic characters and world building. Then they crossed on a stagecoach the gentle and quiet Dutch countryside with its multiple canals, windmills and wooden houses. When they arrived in Rotterdam, the travellers' purse was again empty. A captain, following lengthy negotiations, agreed nevertheless to take them on board. Throughout the whole journey, Shelley talked to a passenger who had conventional ideas about slavery; Mary and Jane supported him dearly. Even though they did not know how they would be able to eat the next day, they trusted that Percy was a genius, and that humankind is perfectible. The sea was as heavy as the day they left England.

20
THE OUTCASTS

On their arrival in London, Shelley could not pay the cab that was transporting their luggage. With Mary, Jane and the luggage, he asked to be driven to his banker, who revealed to him that Harriet had taken all the money in their account. This news provoked the greatest outcry among the two women. The only way for them to get away from this desperate situation without being jailed was to go to visit Harriet herself; Shelley knew her address. He gave it to the cabman, and they went.

Harriet thought at first that her husband was coming back home but got rather shocked when she realised that her rival was waiting at the door. However, she lent them a few pounds, and the three travellers found some poor furnished rooms to stay in.

The situation was desperate. The Godwin family totally refused to see the runaways. Shelley pleaded that he only applied the principles written in *Political Justice*; however, the argument irritated further the author of the essay. *Political Justice* was a theoretical treatise, and its principles could only be valid in the land of Utopia (besides, he had written it a long time ago). But, in London, in a merciless society and even in his own home, to expose him and his only child to his acquaintances' mockery was not acceptable. He would never forgive it.

However, Shelley had borrowed large amounts of money only to lend it to Mary's father.

The bailiffs got at him as soon as they were aware he was back. And worse, not only could Godwin not pay Shelley back, but he also needed more. Godwin had no option but to reply to this perverted and treacherous young man. He did not fail, though, to note in his letters that his conscience was greatly affected.

The double-dealing from the very man he used to admire affected Shelley but also Mary: "Oh, philosophy!" they both said, sighing. As for Mrs Godwin, she simply accused them of having perverted her own child, Jane, and forbade Fanny to ever go and visit them. She went once to visit her daughter, and when she met Shelley in the stairs, she simply turned her head away.

Relations with Harriet were sometimes easy, sometimes difficult, depending on her mood. She did not lack anything really, still having some of Shelley's money and receiving a pension from the old café-keeper, but she was pregnant and very unhappy. She spent her days naively telling her story to the gossips in the neighbourhood or writing to her friend Catherine Nugent, the Dublin dressmaker, in little schoolgirl phrases:

"Every age has its worries. God knows I've got mine. Little Ianthe is well. She's fourteen months old and has six teeth. I don't know what I would have done without my little girl, or even my sister. The world is a place of painful trials for us all. I hardly thought I would have to go through what I have been subject to. But time heals the deepest wounds, and, for my sweet child's sake, I hope to live many more years. Write to me often, please. Let me know how you are. Don't be afraid, although I see nothing to hope for now that virtuous things have become vicious and depraved. That is the way it is. Nothing is permanent in this world. Yet, I suppose there is another world where those who have suffered too much in this one should be happy. Tell me what you think. My sister is with me, and I would like you to know her as I do. She is worthy of your friendship. Farewell, dear friend."

Sometimes, she had hope. Her friends told her that love affairs do not last long and that her husband would one day come back to her; then she felt gay again and wrote to Shelley in an amicable way. She thought it was Mary who did all the wrong, that she had seduced Shelley by telling him unconventional stories, however, he was a good man and would not abandon her and their two children.

At other times, she suffered a flare up of sadness and rage. She tried to make the life of the hated couple difficult; she built up further debts and called the bailiff to Shelley's house; she said that he was actually promiscuous with Godwin's two daughters; she even visited Godwin's bailiffs to alert them and advised them not to have any pity. Mary, who had never met her, said, sighing: "What a terrible woman!"

One day in November, Harriet fainted and thought she was ill. She called first her husband; she sent someone in the middle of the night, and he ran to her. He wanted to stay, without being a lover again, but as the most devoted friend. Harriet did not understand the nuances and as soon he showed eagerness, she became gentle and sweet. But then, he resisted her gently but firmly.

At the end of November, she gave birth to a boy at eight months of pregnancy. Sadly, the birth did not help with reconciliation; Shelley was uncertain about the paternity.

With Mary and despite the hardship, he was still ecstatically happy. They shared the same tastes and were both considering life as a university that could last until old age. They were reading the same books, often out loud to each other's. She went with him to visit the bailiffs or the solicitors. When, on the bank of the Serpentine, just like before in Oxford, he played at launching dinghies made with paper, Mary, sitting by his side, enthusiastically helped him build the fleet.

She started, under his directive, to learn Latin and Greek. Much more cultured than Harriet, she did not see it, like the first Mrs Shelley, as rather annoying play, but as an enhancement of her pleasure. The most charming treat of literature is that it humanises love. Catullus, Theocritus, Petrarch were all joining together to render their kisses even more delightful. Shelley, looking at his new companion studying, admired the strength of her mind and with joy decided that she was much more superior to him.

The presence of Jane, or rather Claire, as Jane had changed the name, she thought ugly for a more romantic one, became the only faint cloud in the house. She was brilliant and charming, but also highly nervous and remarkably sensitive. Nothing was more dangerous for her stress levels than living with a young couple in love. Furthermore, she had a passionate admiration for Shelley and demonstrated it too vividly. Mary started to complain about it. Shelley, on the other end, found these emotional demonstrations neither disagreeable nor shocking.

He hated being alone. When Mary, pregnant, declined joining him for walks or staying up late at night, he welcomed Claire to join him when visiting the bailiff or solicitor, or even walking along the Serpentine, and then asked her to stay up late at night with him. He talked to her about Harriet, Miss Hitchener and his sisters. He enjoyed sharing confidences or a lengthy analysis of his thoughts, and total sincerity seemed to him easier with Claire since she was not his mistress. Soon, Mary showed her discontent. Claire, upset about her sister's criticism, became sombre and silent for a whole day.

In the evening, once Mary had gone upstairs, Shelley tried to calm down Claire. Gently, skilfully and with patience, he talked until midnight about the complicated feeling within their group. His gentle goodwill worked, Claire calmed down and finally stopped being in a sulk. "I have suffered so much," she said. "Imaginary blows, my poor Claire; you interpret words and actions Mary does not care about really". "Even though, I have suffered, I appreciate good people, the ones who do have explanations."

He then went to meet Mary to tell her about the conversation. Above their bedroom they heard Claire walking and talking in her sleep. And then she came and joined them downstairs; she was too nervous and could not stay alone; Mary welcomed her in her bed and Shelley went to bed upstairs.

This little scene repeated itself on and on with only a few variances. Claire's nervousness was affecting Shelley. After having talked all night long about ghosts and appearances of all kinds, they ended up playing at scaring one another. "What is happening to you, Claire?" Shelley asked. "You turned all green… Your eyes… please stop looking at me that way." "You, too, you are so weird… The air is becoming heavy, like it is full of monsters… We should not stay here!"

Then, the moment they said goodnight to each other and went to their respective bedrooms, Shelley and Mary heard a loud cry: a body was rolling downstairs. Claire, with a scared look, told that her pillow had left her bed, pushed away by an invisible hand. Shelley, horrified, listened to her carefully while Mary shrugged her shoulders. She wanted this mad woman to leave.

* * *

The outcasts seldom saw friends. The Boinville-Newton set, in spite of their broad-minded French philosophy, demonstrated some coldness when Shelley told them about his new life. Like for the Godwins, actions did not run on all fours with speech and indulgence in theory allied itself with severity and inclemency in practice.

On the contrary, the sceptics Hogg and Peacock came and joined them at the first call. They trusted Harriet as innocent and did not agree with Shelley's move; however, they were curious and simply viewed passions as comical diseases.

Shelley had not invited Hogg without concerns though; he feared that this cynic would not be liked by his very serious girlfriend. Mary's first impression was not positive actually: "He is funny when he makes a joke," she said, "however, when he starts to talk about a serious subject, it is obvious that his point of view is simply false."

With time, Hogg had become even more British and conservative; he was praising tradition, sport and public schools and was knowledgeable about the good years for port. Finding Mary beautiful and clever, he told Shelley who repeated it to Mary herself. At the next visit, she found him even more friendly than before. Probably, he talked about virtue like he was colour blind, and, in this family of enthusiastic souls, he became the 'inveterate sinner' even though his charm was appreciated. Mary thought that his coldness was a ruse and that actually he was worth more than his words. He was afraid to show sincerity or even to be intense; this would have forced him to deny a thousand things he loved. However, he was far too clever not to feel the weakness of his attitude.

Indeed, helpful and cultured, he was happy to help Mary and Claire to translate Ovid or even Anacreon when their master mysteriously disappeared; thereafter he would even follow them to their milliner without complaining.

Both women were going to the milliner, like poor Harriet was, but with a different spirit. Harriet bought hats with enthusiasm, Mary with a lofty condescension, so that Shelley did not have to excuse in her a concession to fashion which she herself was the first to deplore.

21
THE REAL GODWIN

The house servant brought a letter from a woman who was waiting on the opposite pavement. The letter was from Fanny to alert Shelley that the bailiffs were getting ready to jail him for his debts. Shelley and Claire ran downstairs. Fanny escaped as soon as she saw them. She was afraid of Godwin, who had forbidden her any connection with the outcasts; furthermore, she admired Shelley too much to be able to see him again since he belonged to her sister. Shelley followed, he ran fast and managed to catch her. She told him that the bailiffs were looking for him, that his own editor had given them his address and that Godwin had let it happen.

Without any money to defend himself, Shelley had no option but to disappear. He decided to go and live alone in another place, while Mary and Claire would stay there to foil the enemy's plan. And so, for the first time, the lovers were separated; This was perceived by both as terrible. They ended up meeting in pubs, far away, where they would occasionally exchange stealthy kisses, then quickly leave each other, in case Mary had been followed.

On Sundays, the day when arrests were forbidden and so impossible, they managed to stay together until midnight.

One night, they lost courage. Mary followed Shelley to stay at a miserable inn. The host found it suspicious that this young couple had such very light luggage and denied them a meal before payment. Shelley called Peacock, but then, while waiting for the money, he opened the small book of Shakespeare's work that he always had with him and started to read out loud to Mary *Troilus and Cressida*. This, in turn, made them forget about their hunger for the whole day. The next day, around lunch time, Peacock organised a delivery of cakes.

This life was very difficult indeed, but somehow, they found happiness in suffering together. Hardship and love seemed to mix well, indeed.

When they were far away from each other, while awaiting the protection of the night, they asked a trusted messenger to swiftly exchange written romantic notes.

"O my dearest love," Shelley wrote, "why are our moments of pleasure so short and always interrupted? How long will this last?... Tomorrow, at 3pm near Saint Paul. Please do not forget your love vespers before falling asleep; on my side, I shall not forget my prayers."

"Good night my lover," Mary used to reply, "tomorrow I shall seal this wish on your lips. Dearest and kind creature, press me against you; with all your might, hold your Mary; maybe one day she will find again a father, until then, be everything for me, my love."

* * *

In January 1815, one single event, long waited, transformed this very harsh life. They both reacted without haste or even any hypocritical empathy: the old Sir Bysshe died at the age of 83. Mr Timothy became baronet and Shelley the immediate inheritor.

He left for his father's home in the company of Claire, who was excited and curious. He left her at the village and went alone to the gate of Field- Place. Sir Timothy, inflated by his new title, and even more disgruntled that a baronet could have such a son, requested his butler to stop him at the gate. Shelley sat down on the front steps to read Milton until getting more news. Soon, the doctor went out to tell him that his father was very upset. Then it was the turn of Sydney Shelley to go out to visit the damned son and give him details of the will.

It was an extraordinary will. Indeed, the elder Sir Bysshe was determined to constitute a large fortune for his inheritance, and for that to increase the entailed estate as much as he could. He was leaving £240,000, of which £80,000 constituted Percy's entitlement on the death of his father; the rest was free. However, Sir Bysshe requested that this was combined with the £80,000 to create a large amount which could be transmitted from first-born son to the next over generations of Shelley baronets in the future. For this, the agreement and signature of his grandson was required, and he thought of buying him as follows: if Shelley consented to prolong the entailed estate, he could have the benefit of the whole wealth; if not, he would inherit only after the death of his father the £80,000, which could never be taken away from him.

Shelley went back to London meditating about this odd news and went to see his lawyer to discuss it. He felt he could not agree with the prolongation of the entailed estate, since he fundamentally disagreed with this plutocratic lawmaking. In any case, he had no desire, neither for himself nor for his future children, for ownership of enormous wealth. What he wished for was to have as soon as possible enough money to live as he wished, together with a small amount of money to pay his debts. He sent a proposal to his father, which was to sell his rights against an immediate set-up of an annuity. This combination pleased Sir Timothy, who, giving up trying to make Shelley submit, was actually thinking about his second son; sadly, lawyers were unsure this was possible within the terms of the will. They only agreed with the sale by Shelley of his inheritance from a great uncle. From that, Shelley got an annuity of £1,000 a year and received £3,000-£4,000 to pay off his debts; it was not a large amount of money. However, it meant for Shelley the end of misery, of furnished rooms and of bailiff's visits.

His first idea was to allow an annuity for Harriet. He promised £200 a year. This added to her father's annuity should keep her out of trouble. Then, he decided to help with Godwin's debts and invested his whole first annuity for this project.

The venerable friend found the offer of £1,000 much below what he was expecting. Listening to him, there was nothing easier than borrowing from an inheritance close to thousands and thousands of pounds, amount which was so needed for Skinner's library in the first place.

Shelley, exasperated, yet still polite, was staggered, and even outraged, that Mary's father was still writing to his daughter's abductor to ask for money, while at the same time declining any relationship with his daughter, who suffered as the result of this weakness of character. Godwin replied it was because he was asking for money from her abductor that he could not see his daughter; his dignity would not permit it. In fact, he could not risk that people could infer that he traded his own daughter's honour against the payment of his debt. His scruples made him so strong that he even returned a cheque made out in his name, signalling that decency dictated that both names, Shelley and Godwin, could not appear on the same cheque. Shelley could write a cheque for Mr Smith or even Mr Hume. He would then accept it. Further letters were exchanged as follows:

Shelley to Godwin:

"Sir, I must admit not to understand how the current financial agreement between us leads you to restrict your conduct towards me. This agreement did not even exist at the time of our return from France. Even though, your attitude was the same. In my view, neither I, nor your daughter, deserve the punishment we are receiving. It has always appeared to me that it should be your duty, as the person with such a substantial opinion, to ensure that a young, innocent and devoted couple with evident goodwill should not be likened to a prostitute and a seducer. I am both extremely astonished and shocked, especially since I realised that you seemed selfishly ready to reconnect with us, for you, your family and your creditors, despite how we previously inspired in you such horror. Furthermore, neither my misery nor the hardship I suffered for your sake have prompted your reconciliation with us. Please, do not ask any more for apologies, because my blood is now boiling in my veins, and my heart is jumping at the sight of any human form or shape, when I think of the contempt and hostility that I, your benefactor and fervent friend, has indeed received from you and from humankind."

Godwin to Shelley:

"… I am sorry to have to tell you that your letter is written in a style inconsistent with reconciliation. As such, if I was replying with the same tone, we would end up in a sour dispute with no end; while I remain intelligent and emotional, I will never cease to consider your action as the greatest sadness in my entire life."

Shelley to Godwin:

"From now on, we shall limit our communication to business only. I agree with you that I should borrow on my annuities. I understand clearly how necessary immediate advances are for you. I shall do anything in my power to obtain them."

The borrower was not discouraged by the cold contempt.

22
THE CONQUEST OF DON JUAN

Mary's baby was born prematurely. The doctor told them that he would not live. Shelley kept watch between the cradle and the bed in the company of Titus Livy and Seneca. Fanny brought baby clothes from the fickle Mrs Godwin. However, the philosopher remained inflexible. Hogg came to talk and told them about the big news of the moment, the return of Napoleon from the island of Elba, and made Mary smile with his sense of humour. Being feverish and pregnant in the company of Shelley, she had felt as if she were in some way evading real life; Hogg was more tangible and real.

Despite the predictions, the baby survived; he lived on. Mary started to be positive and confident as a mother, when sadly, one morning, she found him dead. This caused immense grief.

Shelley and Claire carried on going together to various meetings all around London; Mary stayed at home thinking of her little child. "I used to be a mother, and now I am no more," she repeated to herself. At night, she dreamed that the baby was still alive, and that she could reanimate him by rubbing him near the fire. Then she would wake up; the cradle was empty. From the street, noises from the crowd and shouting could be heard. It was indeed the time of riots. Threats of war were coming from France too. Mary had forever a veil of tears in front of her eyes.

She became even more exasperated by the presence of Claire at home. She was certain of Claire's love for Shelley. However, Percy's loyalty was evident to her; his morality was more than human, angelic even; but he naively thought he could read Petrarch to a passionate girl, to direct her studies and reading, and stay up all night talking to her without her getting excited. "It is like my charming Shelley know more about elves than women."

At night, when finally, alone with him, she admitted her feelings of jealousy. He did not judge fairly the feeling of jealousy and even considered it low and unworthy of his divine Mary. He felt that his own capacity for love was infinite, and that he did not withdraw anything from his lover by protecting another woman. The company of this brilliant and wild being was so important to him. However, he agreed that the state of their threesome had become in many ways oppressive and unsustainable.

Finally, Mary begged him to ask Claire, now referred as 'your friend', to leave. They looked for a position for her as a governess or housekeeper; however, the reputation they had gained after their sudden flight to France made any enquiries very difficult indeed.

However, Claire did not think at all about leaving. She was delighted with this intellectual intimacy and waited, unconcerned, for further developments, whatever they might be.

Finally, Mary's kind firmness won. It was decided that Claire would leave for the seaside to stay with a widow who was a friend of the Godwins.

(Mary's diary:)

"Friday. Not at ease really, following breakfast, read Spencer; Shelley is going out with his friend; he comes back first. Translation of *Ovid*, ninety lines. Jefferson is coming; I read my *Ovid*. Shelley and the lady are going out: after tea, last discussion between Shelley and his friend."

"Saturday. Claire is leaving, Shelley, her escort; Jefferson will come only after five. Worry not to see Shelley coming back, go out to meet him. It is raining. He comes back at six-thirty in the evening, the story ends. Read *Ovid*. Charles Clairmont comes for tea. We speak about paintings. I am starting a new diary for our new start in life."

* * *

For a few days, Claire, exiled in the countryside, first appreciated the calm following the recent stormy period, but she was not a girl to be satisfied for long with a solitary and quiet life in the countryside; she resolved to find a reason for living and she found it.

Lovers often think so wrongly and tend to believe that it was meeting an exceptional being that triggered love. The truth is that love pre-exists and leads one to look for its purpose and if not found, to make one create it anew. While this phenomenon is unconscious for a reserved person, for Claire, a daring woman, she knew clearly that since she could not rob Shelley from her sister, she must quickly find a replacement and another hero as the purpose of her unemployed feelings. Alone in the countryside, she could not find anyone. Some lovers-to-be in such a situation usually start to write to soldiers or famous actors. But she was literate and so, she looked for a poet.

She did not find any other suitor other than George Gordon, namely Lord Byron, the most hated and loved man in England of the time. She knew his poems by heart. Shelley read them often and with much enthusiasm; she was aware of the stories told about his perversion, his diabolical charm and his maddening, cruel nature.

The beauty of the man, the grandeur of his title, the genius behind the author, the ardour of his ideas, the stories of his scandalous love affairs: everything coalesced to make him a hero. He already had several noble mistresses: the Countess of Oxford, Lady Frances Webster, and poor Lady Caroline Lamb who, the first day she saw him, wrote in her journal: "Mad, bad and dangerous to know", and then just below: "However, my destiny is now contained in this beautiful and pale face."

Byron had married and all London was gossiping that after the ceremony, when entering the wedding car, he said to his new wife: "Now you are my wife, I have sufficient grounds to hate you; if at least you were someone else's woman, I could try and love you." He then treated her with so much contempt, that she asked for a divorce less than a year later. Scandalmongers spread the word that she had discovered an incestuous relationship between Byron and his sister Augusta. As this rumour spread, horrified and more timid souls retreated well away from him.

But the truth was that Claire was attracted by difficulties and trusted her ingenuity; she managed to obtain her new Don Juan's home address and decided to take a chance.

Claire to Byron:

"This is a stranger who risks writing to you. I am not asking for charity, because I do not need any: I tremble with fear when I think of the fate of this letter. If you see me as an annoyance, who could blame you? You might find it odd, however, that I wish to place my happiness in your hands. If a woman with an unstained reputation, free from her father's oversight and without any husband, if this woman was telling you, her heart beating fast, that she has loved you for years, and if she ensures secrecy and safety, if she is ready to reply to you with goodwill and remain unfailingly devoted, could you betray her or could you remain as quiet as the grave? I want a response from you without delay; please, write to me with the name E. Trefusis, Noley Place, Marylebone."

Don Juan did not reply. This unknown woman with such a pompous style was a small fry or the noble lord. However, what could be more tenacious than a woman tired of her virtue? Claire attacked a second time:

"Lord Byron is asked to reply if he could, this very evening at seven pm, welcome a lady who most desires to communicate to him some very important information; she asks to be received alone and in secret."

Lord Byron told his servant to reply that he was not in London.

Thereafter, Claire wrote under her own name; she wanted to work at the theatre; she knew that Lord Byron was in charge of the Theatre Royal Drury Lane and needed some advice from him. This time, Byron replied to her that she should contact the director. Not at all thrown off by the reply, she immediately changed her course of action; she was not interested anymore in the theatre but in literature;

she had already written half a novel and would very much like Lord Byron to look at her attempt. Since he kept silent or limited his replies to a few words, she risked making the precise offer no man with any pride would deny.

"I may seem to you careless or even perverted; however, there is only one thing in the world that time will demonstrate to you: that I love with kindness and affection, that I am incapable of revenge or even of any kind of stratagem… I can assure you that I see your future just like mine.

"Could you be opposed to the following plan? One evening, both of us leave and drive as far as ten or twelve miles from London. There, we shall be incognito and free; then, you could go back the next day. I have organised everything to prevent any suspicion whatsoever. Would you please allow me to live with you for only a few hours?... Where? I shall not stay longer and shall leave as soon as you say so… And then, do whatever you want; go anyplace you wish; you can refuse to see me ever again; even behave badly; whatever, I shall only recall your manners and the wild mysteriousness of your behaviour."

And then, finally, Don Juan, stalked and tired of this obstinate courting, finally accepted. In any case, he was ready to leave England to go and live in Switzerland or Italy, and the certainty of an imminent departure conveniently mitigated this romantic constraint.

23

ARIEL AND DON JUAN

However, Don Juan had not considered Elvira's energy. Claire decided to follow him to Switzerland. This girl with the olive skin was a force of nature. She had already planned to be chaperoned by the Shelleys, who she thought were ready to accept a new departure.

Since she had left them, they had settled on the bank of the Thames, near Windsor. Under the Park's magnificent oak trees, Shelley wrote his first great work following *Queen Mab*; it was a poem: *Alastor, or The Spirit of Solitude* and was about his own story, slightly modified though; the style was quite different from what he had written before; the religious and moral theories, still the subject of his writing, were only referred to here in the background, with here and there the emergence of poetic descriptions of beautiful landscapes.

In the foreword, he explained that if he had now abandoned his student hobbyhorse, he did not regret any of his past actions and still preferred this painful learning curve to Hogg's comfortable renunciation:

> "Those who do not risk any mistakes, who do not feel hungry for knowledge, even if it is dubious, who do not

have any venerable superstition; those who do not like anything on this planet and are not looking for any hope for infinity; those who stay with contempt away from friendship, who do not rejoice at simple joys, who do not cry in face of a human being's hardship; those people and their look-a-likes have their fair part of malediction… They are morally dead. They are neither friends, nor lovers, neither fathers nor citizens of the world, neither benefactors of their country… they live a useless life and are just getting ready for a miserable grave"

However, even if Shelley did not regret anything, the stay in England was becoming unbearable. Mary, his companion but not his spouse, was suffering from nearly total social isolation. She started to think that maybe, in a foreign country where her adventure was not known, she would have more opportunities to meet friends and acquaintances.

Mary bore a second child, who fortunately stayed alive. He was a beautiful little boy.

She named him William, like Godwin. The household was becoming consequential with the addition of a wet nurse, a burden on the still meagre pension. It was known that life in Switzerland was much cheaper. Claire did not do much to convince her.

Like the time of their first escape, but with more comfort, the odd trio went across Paris, Burgundy, the Jura mountains and reached the *Hotel d'Angleterre* in Sècheron, near Geneva. The hotel was by the lake; from the windows, they could see the lapping blue waves twinkling with the sun's rays. Under a luminous veil, the darkened mountain line shimmered; far away, they could make out white peaks resembling a glistening, solid cloud. Having escaped London's winter, these sunny landscapes appeared appealing and pleasant to them, and so they decided to rent a boat and stayed a few days on the lake, reading and sleeping.

* * *

As their youthful group was living as if they had been forgotten between the ground and the sky, Childe Harold, with a sumptuous carriage, crossed the plains of Flanders to reach and join them.

One must say that England, at that time of crisis, had contradictory values. Its people, who were already well-known for their most astonishing tolerance, had banished Lord Byron because of a supposed incestuous relationship with his sister. One day, when Byron arrived at a ball, all the women flew out of the room, as if he were the devil himself. So, he decided to leave forever this hypocritical country.

His departure triggered the most passionate curiosity. People, who often punish drastically expressions of human instinct, in truth admire and envy them. In Dover, when the migrant boarded, at least two lines of spectators ran alongside him towards the passenger ramp; many ladies borrowed and dressed up in their servants' clothing to mix with the crowd. They pointed out to each other his enormous resting bed, library and porcelain crockery.

During the crossing, the sea was rough. Lord Byron reminded his companions that his grandfather, Admiral Byron, had been known by the name of Jack the Tempest, because he never boarded without a gust of wind blowing up. He took a certain satisfaction in imagining himself following the sombre destiny of his family. Feeling melancholy, he wanted his own hardship to be significant.

* * *

A few days later, an unusual activity animated the hotel in Sècheron: a commotion around the arrival of the illustrious lord. Despite her audacity, Claire was restless and quite nervous, Shelley happy, yet impatient. Neither the accusation about an incestuous relationship, nor the relationship between Claire and Byron could shock him or drive him away. On the contrary, he was hoping for a romantic relationship between Byron and his sister-in-law; that is, for them to be as happy as he was with Mary. And as for Byron's reported incest, he could see no natural arguments against a brother loving his sister. The law forbade it as the mere result of human societies indulging absurd fantasies. He even found the idea one of the most poetic possible. And as for Mary, she was happy to find Claire finally neutralised, even within a quite dangerous situation.

The first meeting with Byron was far from disappointing. The beauty of his face was striking. One was first struck first by the air of proud intelligence, then by a moon-like pallor from which two animated and sombre big eyes sparkled with a velvety gaze. His hair was dark and slightly wavy, and his eyebrow line was perfect. Both nose and chin were gracefully shaped by pure strength. The only flaw within this beautiful being showed up when he was walking. One said he had a clubbed foot. Byron himself referred to his split foot, as he enjoyed feeling diabolical, rather than disabled. Mary felt that his limp triggered in him a kind of shyness; each time he had to walk towards some spectators, he hurled satanic phrases. On the register, he wrote 100 for his age.

Both men appreciated one another; Byron saw Shelley as an aristocrat, who despite his misery, retained the charming ease of those young members of English high society. He was astounded by Shelley's high culture; even if he himself had read a lot, he had not done it with such seriousness. Shelley wanted to know, while Byron wanted to dazzle and captivate. Byron was aware of this. He immediately felt that

Shelley's willpower was a pure, taut strength, while his own fluttered according to his passions and mistresses.

Shelley, unassuming, could not see Byron's admiration, which was carefully hidden. When listening to the third canto of *Childe Harold's Pilgrimage*, he became emotional and discouraged. Its strength and powerful rhythm, its irresistible flowing movement were the marks of the prodigy, Shelley despaired of ever matching it.

If he felt enthusiasm for the poet, the man surprised him a great deal. He was expecting a titan in revolt; he found a wounded lord, preoccupied by the joys and pain of vanity. This appeared to Shelley as childish, really. Byron defied prejudice, but still seemed to believe in it. His desires had faced prejudice and he ignored it, but he still regretted his actions. Shelley's actions were naïve, Byron acted in full consciousness. Rejected by society, he only loved worldly success. A bad husband, he respected only legitimate union. He expressed cynical views for revenge, rather than because of conviction. Between perversion and marriage, he could not conceive any possible middle ground. He was trying to terrify England by playing a game full of audacity, but this was out of despair because he had not been able to conquer it in a traditional role.

Shelley was looking for some form of exaltation in his relationships with women. On the other hand, Byron was looking for an excuse to entertain. Shelley was angelical, he adored woman; Byron, basically human, only too human, desired them while despising them in his speech. He used to say: 'What is terrible with women, is that one cannot leave neither with nor without them." or "I could love a woman who has enough intelligence to know that she has to admire me, but not enough to need to be admired in return."

As a result of their brief conversations, Byron unwittingly took on the role of Don Juan and unexpectedly revealed Shelley's hidden mysticism.

This did not prevent them appreciating each other. When his friend, like a fisherman searching for souls, was attempting to convince him about a complicated concept or a big question, Byron tried to defend himself with brilliant paradoxes, which Shelley the artist appreciated as much as Shelley the moralist condemned them.

Both men were passionate about sailing. They purchased a boat, and most evening sailed away, accompanied by Mary, Claire and the young doctor Polidori. Byron and Shelley, in silence, rested their oars to gaze at the sky, its clouds and the moon's reflection in the hope of spotting any fleeting images. Claire sang and her beautiful and clear voice led their thoughts in a voluptuous flight above the star-spangled waters.

One evening when there was bad weather, Byron ignoring and defying the storm, started to sing an Albanian melody: "Be sentimental," he said, "and give me your full attention!" He then gave a long, croaky call, and laughed. From that day, Mary and Claire named him 'the Albanian', and 'Albe' for short.

Shelley and Byron went for a literary pilgrimage around the lake. They visited the places where Rousseau had set his *Nouvelle Heloise* story: "Clarens, sweet Clarens, birthplace of deep love", Gibbon's Lausanne and of course Ferney-Voltaire. Shelley's enthusiasm intoxicated Byron, who wrote as a result some of his most beautiful verses. Near Meillerie, a violent storm nearly capsized the boat. Byron started getting undressed and prepared. Shelley, who did not know how to swim, remained impassive, his arms crossed. His obvious courage increased Byron's esteem for him but he kept it quieter than ever.

The Shelleys, tired of being at the hotel, rented at Coligny a cottage on the lake; Byron settled in the Diodati villa, up the hill. A vineyard separated the two homes. One morning, local winemakers saw Claire run out of the villa to the Shelleys' cottage, losing one of her shoes. Ashamed to be seen, she did not stop to collect it; the good Swiss winemakers, all jeering, took the lost shoe of the English maid to the village's town hall.

For Byron, it was not a happy love story. Claire was pregnant and Byron, already tired of her, brutally expressed his lassitude towards her. He may have had admired once her voice and mind; however, she had rapidly become quite annoying. Furthermore, he did not feel any duty towards this girl who had offered herself to him with such tenacity:

"Abducted?... Who got abducted in the first place other than I?... One accuses me of being harsh with women, when I have been their victim my whole life. Since Troy, nobody has been abducted other than me."

Shelley went to talk to him about Claire and his child to be.

According to Claire, the noble Lord was not interested in her at all, and had only one desire, which was to get rid of her and never see her again. It was a position Shelley could not fight against. However, he wanted and tried to protect the rights of the child-to-be.

Strangely, Byron thought first about entrusting the child to his sister Augusta, despite their publicly known scandalous union. Claire refused categorically, then, he proposed to look after the baby himself from the age of one on the condition he become the only responsible adult.

For the Shelleys, it was becoming difficult to stay with him. It was not that the two men were in conflict; rather, Shelley was starting to find the negotiations painful and tiresome. Claire was suffering, though, and Mary was shocked by Byron's attitude and his cynical point of view. When he used to say that women should not eat at the men's table, that their place was either in the serial or pregnant and well-guarded, Mary Wollstonecraft's daughter boiled inside.

Soon, Mary became nostalgic for the lush English countryside. A home bordering an English river seemed to her such a delicious refuge.

Shelley wrote to his friends, Peacock and Hogg, and asked them to rent such a house for them. They were back travelling.

* * *

Following their departure, Byron wrote to his sister Augusta:

"Please, do not reprimand me. What could I have done, really? A dangerous girl, despite what I said or did, decided to follow me, or rather to herald me, since I found her on my arrival. I had all the trouble in the world to convince her to go. Finally, she left….

"Now, my dearest, I will tell you that, in truth, I just could not prevent it, that I have done everything I could and that I have managed to end the story. I do not love her. In truth, I do not have any love left for anyone really; however, you will understand, I could not behave as a stoic with a woman who travelled eight hundred miles to stop me being philosophical… So, now you are aware of what I know about the whole affair. This story is over."

Shelley kept writing to Byron and did not forget about his friend's salvation. He wrote to him with respect for the great poet mixed with an almost tangible haughtiness towards the man he saw as lacking character. Faced with Byron's constant concern about his reputation, success and the London gossip, he countered with true glory:

> "Is it nothing to create greatness and goodness, and focus on the possible infinite expansions? Is it nothing to have become a source from which other human beings shall extract beauty and strength?... What would be the human race if Homer or even Shakespeare had not written anything?... It is not about advising you to aim for glory, not at all. Rather, the aim of your work should be more focused and simpler. You should only desire to express your own ideas, to address them to those who are capable of thinking like you. Glory follows those it is unworthy to guide."

Thereafter, Lord Byron headed on to Venice, the carefree city. It was there that he read these demands and urging with a great lassitude. He was tired of having to earn esteem.

24
SEPULCHRE IN THE GARDEN FOR LOVE

Of the three young girls who used to bring joy to the house in Skinner Street, only one remained. It was Fanny Imlay. Although she was the daughter of neither Mr nor Mrs Godwin, Fanny was still living at Skinner Street. She used to call them mother and father; she was so gentle. However, she was the only one who had not found a lover or husband. She was cautious, shy and full of principles: all virtues that men praise but rarely reward. One day, she thought she could appeal to Shelley and started writing to him, her heart beating heavily while exchanging intimate thoughts. However, Mary's hazelnut eyes abolished any hopes that Fanny had not yet allowed to take full shape.

In this home, now deserted and constantly bothered by financial issues, Mrs Godwin, quite upset, bullied her as a kind of revenge. On his part, Godwin tried to make out that he could no longer financially care for her and that she would soon need to find some work. Fanny was hoping to find something, too, and thought of becoming a professor. However, Mary and Jane's escape was still talked about, and, clearly, most of schools' headteachers simply did not want to deal with this family anymore.

From afar, Fanny admired with both envy and sadness the mad and adventurous life of her sisters. She wished so much to be in Geneva, walking round the lake, sometimes in the company of the famous Lord Byron, the poet so much talked about in London!

"Is he as handsome as in his portrait? Tell me if he has an agreeable voice, because this is so appealing to me. Does he come to see you as a neighbour, without any ceremony, just like friends? I would like so much to understand if he is capable of having done what these gossip hawkers, only attracted by the scandal, are accusing him of. Reading his poetry, I cannot believe him to be so awful. Please, reply to my questions; when I like a poet, I would so much like to respect the man. Sailing with both Shelley and Byron must have been so delightful. I would like so much to read the verses the poet wrote at the place where Julie drowned. When will they be published in England? Could I receive the manuscript by any chance? Tell him that you have a friend, who does not have much joy in her live and wishes to read it so much…"

Mary, Claire and Shelley received these charming letters with pity, yet with an air of superiority. Poor Fanny! How can she stay at Skinner Street! How can she still believe that Godwin's writing and financial issues, complicated by Mrs Godwin's rage, were the most important issues in the world!

The two young women had an acute feeling of freedom, thinking of Fanny's state of slavery. They valued even more their respective love stories in the face of her solitude. Before leaving Geneva, Shelley and Mary went and bought a watch for her, a snobbish gift.

On their arrival back in England, they went to settle in Bath and met her while passing through London. She was sad, and only spoke about her isolation and feeling useless. When they left, with a trembling voice, she said goodbye to Shelley. She then wrote to him the same candid letters as before, with a kind of vaguely disapproving tone, the very tone people already forgotten by others use to address those who are full of life.

Meanwhile, Godwin, who had been forced to stop a project because of further financial issues, became even more sour-tempered. And to aggravate things, one aunt, who had initially offered to welcome Fanny into her school, subsequently let everybody know that Mary and Claire's sister would only scare the mothers of the high society.

One morning, the Shelleys received a strange letter, in which Fanny wrote her farewells to them in quite mysterious terms: "I am leaving for a place from which I hope to never ever come back from."

Mary asked Shelley to immediately leave for Bristol. He came back without any news; he went there again the next day, but this time came back quite devastated.

Fanny had taken the Swansea stagecoach to take a room at the town's inn: there, she had retired to her room, saying to the maid that she was tired. The next day, she did not come downstairs. The hosts decided to open her door of the room, where they found her corpse. Her long hair covered her young face. She was wearing the watch that Shelley and Mary had given her. On the table there was a bottle of laudanum, together with the beginning of a letter:

> "A long time ago, I made the decision that there is no better option than ending the life of a being born under an unlucky star, a being who had brought people only difficulties and a worsening of their own health by raising this very being. It is possible that you will be hurt by hearing about my death, but soon, you shall gratefully forget that once there was a creature named…"

Godwin had written in *Political Justice* that suicide was not a crime, and that the only issue was to decide if the social benefit of years of future life would prevent the wish for death. Following the tragic event, he wrote for the first time to his daughter Mary since her escape. The purpose of his letter was to order the outcasts to remain silent about Fanny's death, as this could only further harm the family's reputation.

* * *

Fanny's terrible death affected Shelley a great deal; the charitable Mrs Godwin had suggested to her that she should take her own life because of her unconfessed love for him. He indeed recalled a few emotional sins he previously ignored and started to feel guilty about having always considered Fanny as being of lower order. Maybe, without knowing, he had himself triggered her love when, abandoned by Harriet, he had been looking for care and reassurance from any female tenderness. It is possible she had tried anxiously to find a sign from him, but had found only detachment, or even complacency: "It is so difficult to understand the other's soul! How much suffering one can induce, without knowing! How easy it is not to realise the other's deep feelings, even feelings of despair, without any hint of suspicion for it."

And so, it was not sufficient to be sincere and to have only honest intentions. One can hurt as much by lack of perception as by nastiness. He felt even more sad and despaired as he thought about it.

To shake off his sadness, he went to pay a visit, all alone, to the young critic Leigh Hunt, who talked about his poetry with such clever enthusiasm. Leigh Hunt lived near London, in a little town hidden by a large forest, where the smoke above the roofs, fields and trees created an urban, yet bucolic site. His wife, Marianne, was both humble and literate; he had many children with whom Shelley was able to play. There he could partly forget Fanny and Godwin. The visit was short, but delightful. He came back full of energy.

On his return, he found a letter from Hookham. He hastened to open it. He had asked the publisher to find Harriet, whom he had not heard from for the past two months. She had collected her pension in March and September; however, from October, nobody knew where she was.

"My dear sir," Hookham wrote, "it has been nearly a month since I received your letter. You must be surprised that I did not reply before; I was wishing to, however, I had great difficulties finding your requested information about Mrs Shelley and your children. I was still trying to find her address when someone came to inform me about her death by suicide. As you might suspect, I first did not trust the news. I went to see a friend of Mr Westbrook. The truth was inescapable. Her corpse has been found and recovered from the depths of the water last Tuesday. The magistrates who examined the body did not get any further information. The conclusion was short: 'found drowned'… Your children are well and, I think, are still in London."

Shelley left for London in a very bad state. He imagined with horror the beautiful, blonde and childlike head, which in the past had looked at him with so much joy, now soiled by the darkest mud of the river and possibly deformed by the greenish swelling of a drowned corpse. He speculated a thousand times about the reasons behind this choice of a horrible death and the abandonment of her children.

In London, his friends, Leigh Hunt and Hookham, received him with care and went through what they heard. In *The Times*, a short article said:

> "On Tuesday, the corpse of a woman of respectable appearance and pregnant was found in the Serpentine. She wore an expensive ring. A want of honour in her own conduct is supposed to have led to this fatal catastrophe, her husband being abroad."

In the district, the gossips of the district were about everything they knew: Harriet had not received letters from her husband because her previous landlady never forwarded them to her. Harriet then lost any hope of ever seeing her husband coming back and let herself down by her desperate conduct. She first lived with an officer, who then had to leave her to go to the colonies with his regiment. Then, incapable of bearing her solitude, she went to live with a low-life protector, a groom, people said. Westbrook's family took the children, but then refused to receive her at their home. She was pregnant, isolated, and terrified by the scandalous situation she was in. Then, the corpse in the river…

Shelley had a terrible night… In a state of advanced pregnancy… this end of life… this madness… Most the intimate memories of his life with Harriet came back to him, recreating in his vivid imagination the likely last moments of her life. Harriet in love, Harriet scared, Harriet in despair: states of mind he knew too well. This name, which had meant for so many years the whole universe to him, it was now necessary to associate this very name with low life and degrading situations. "Harriet, my wife, a prostitute! Harriet, my wife, now dead by drowning… "

Sometimes, he asked himself if in fact he was responsible for it. He rejected firmly this idea, though: "I did what I had to; each time, I have done what I believed the most loyal, and I have never been interested or selfish. When I left her, we did not love each other anymore. Thereafter, I have cared for her, according to or even above my means. I have never been harsh with her, only the odious Westbrooks… and should I have sacrificed my life and my senses to a mediocre and unfaithful wife?"

His reasoning led him to 'no'; his friends Hogg and Peacock, who were supporting him with great care, also replied 'no'. He asked them to repeat it, as he sometimes was drawn towards believing there had been a mysterious and super-human duty that he had failed. "In breaking up traditional connections, one can free mysterious human forces, which can make people act without anyone knowing and lead to terrible consequences… Freedom is good only for a strong mind, for those who have a sense of honour, and Harriet was a simple and tiny soul. A poor drowned woman, childlike and blond head."

In the morning, he wrote a kind letter to Mary, who he saw as a different person having in contrast a serene gentleness. He asked her to welcome his two young children, Ianthe and Charles.

His lawyer then informed Shelley that the Westbrooks planned to oppose him caring for them because of his religious opinions, and that they thought that his free union with Miss Godwin was inappropriate for the education of the children.

25
THE RULES OF THE GAME

Can a wedding add anything to the happiness of confident lovers? The event proved that it can at least transform the face of a conceited person. Godwin showed off with immense satisfaction when he heard that his daughter was to become respectable as the future Lady Shelley; yet he ended up inspiring even more contempt in his previous disciple.

For several days though, they all wonder if it was actually acceptable to celebrate the wedding just days following Harriet's death. However, the experts of worldly conventions confirmed that one should not wait any longer to celebrate by the church a union already blessed twice by nature.

Two weeks after the corpse of the first Lady Shelley was removed from the Serpentine, a priest united Mary and Percy at the church of St Mildred, Bread Street, in the presence of Mr Godwin, preening himself and the affected and glorious Mrs Godwin. In the evening, for the first time since their escape, the Shelleys had dinner at Skinner Street.

However, the family party atmosphere was very sad, held in the small dining room where both Fanny and Harriet had spent time during their short life. The shadows of the desperate, depressed and dissatisfied were present to torment those still living. It is true that Godwin's past rage had been replaced by an excessive urbanity since the morning ceremony. However, too many background memories haunted the guests, making cordiality quite impossible.

That evening, Mary wrote in her diary with all simplicity:

"Travel to London. A wedding has taken place. I am reading Chesterfield and Locke."

Mary had a strong spirit; the petite drowned wife could never match it.

* * *

The official wedding resolved at least one legal issue: the previous argument of free union, used by those who denied Shelley's rights regarding his children, had just lost its validity. However, the Westbrook family refused to change their position. Through the retired coffee-shop owner's words, both the children, Ianthe and Charles Shelley, wrote to the chancellor:

"Our father has publicly declared his atheism and has published an ungodly title with the name: *Queen Mab*, and even another work, where he clearly denied the existence of a creator, the sanctity of marriage and all sacred principles of morality."

For these reasons, the virtuous, precocious little children were clearly requesting not to be educated by such a dishonourable father, but rather by people with high morality chosen by the court: for example, their maternal grandfather and the amiable aunt Eliza.

The lawyer, anticipating the Lord Chancellor's probable beliefs, did not risk any argument in defence of *Queen Mab*. He only tried to minimise the impact of a book that was written at the age of nineteen:

> "In spite of Shelley's strong arguments against marriage, Shelley got married twice even before he was twenty-five! As soon as he was free from the despotic rules of the links he wrote about with such horror and contempt, he created more and consented to be again a victim. We hope that such obvious differences between his opinions and acts will help the Lord Chancellor to not take seriously this immature writing."

About trusting the children to their maternal family, he wrote:

> "We should point out that Mr John Westbrook does not have any skills for the education of Lord Shelley's children. And as for Miss Westbrook, the arguments are even stronger; she is illiterate and vulgar, and worse, it is because of her advice that Shelley, at only nineteen,

kidnapped the once seventeen-year-old Miss Harriet Westbrook. Elisabeth, the proposed tutor, was thirty, and if she had behaved correctly, as a trusty and friendly guardian of her sister, so much hardship and dishonour could have been prevented for the two families involved."

The lawyer's acumen and his plan for his client's success, by denigrating the opinions of his youth, appeared to Shelley as an insufferable hypocrisy. He wrote to the Lord Chancellor that his beliefs about marriage had not changed at all, and even if he had to behave according to rules and customs, he was not renouncing the freedom of being able to be critical.

The Lord Chancellor's secretaries registered the following:

"We are dealing with a father who expects, because of his intellectual and analytical skills, a moral and virtuous duty from those he is responsible for to follow a way of life considered as immoral and perverted by the law in the first place… Under those circumstances, I cannot leave children under his responsibility."

However, the Lord Chancellor did not leave them under the authority of the despicable Westbrooks; on the contrary he asked Doctor Hume, a military physician already involved in the education of Charles, to prepare him to enter a reputable school led by an orthodox clergyman. As for little Ianthe, she was to be educated by Mrs Hume, who would ensure that she prayed every morning and before each meal and read many good books, even an expunged Shakespeare; all this for £100 per child. Mr Shelley would be allowed to visit them twice a year, but always with a chaperone; Mr Westbrook would be able to see them at any time and alone if he wished to.

Shelley was very badly affected by this sentence. In some way, it sanctioned officially, even in a mild and apparently reasonable manner, his exile from civilised society. It was like the certification of incurable madness.

* * *

During the court case, he bought a house near the beautiful town of Marlow. Ariel had finally agreed to live in a human home. A large gallery was transformed into a library, decorated by casts of Venus and Apollo. The garden was grand; a little girl of exceptional beauty played with William and Clara Shelley: it was Alba, the daughter of Claire and Byron. Her father was still in Venice where, some said, he was enjoying life. Claire received little news from him.

The recent hardship had marked Shelley's face. He grew thinner, feverish and more bowed. An acute pain on his side prevented him from sleeping. The doctors, unable to cure it, diagnosed it as of nervous origin.

His mood was sombre indeed. Life had brought so much hardship; his good intentions had become the reason for so much misery that he started to hate any plans or actions. He felt a confused but strong need to separate himself from a group of humans he despised: those with erratic reactions and terrible passions. The real world appeared to him so deceitful that he only wished to deal with love and hate within a closed docile and malleable world. Ideas for poems, still empty and vague, fluttered like shadows around him, fed both by sadness and daydreaming, and jeopardised his strength for action.

These aerial creations, these crystalline palaces, which, with their light mists, had hidden life from him, gradually loosened, as if by an invisible force. They were not dispelled; on the contrary, gentle rocked, they rose up in all their glory towards the high regions of pure poetry. From there, Shelley perceived the world of the living: the dark brown earth, hard to cultivate, the harsh faces of men, the anxious and sensitive women, a world tough and cruel from which he would have liked so much to be able to escape.

The poem he often thought of was about an ideal revolution. He did not want any bloody or gory scenes, which made reading about the French Revolution very difficult, even though beautiful. He imagined that his revolution could be the creation of two lovers. His own experience showed him that only a woman's love could inspire great courage.

His idyllic anarchists, Laon and his lover Cythna, were inspired by himself and Mary. He would make them climb the stake to die for their ideas, just what he wished for his own death, with a last kiss surrounded by flames, so special that the actual torment could be transformed by a sophisticated refinement of the senses. For him, love could only reach its full power when associated with shared ideas and suffering. Now that he and Mary were married, that they had some money making the life much easier, he only thought about escaping this mundane and boring happiness and imagined the perilous and magnificent destiny which could have been his, in another time, or another country.

He used to go to work on the small islets of the Thames, inhabited only by swans, and, lying down in a boat surrounded by high reeds, he scrutinised the sky for images. Contemplating the sky's constant and subtle changes brought him so much pleasure; every day, he felt even more that his real mission on Earth was to take hold of the most fleeting nuances and to fix them with words as light and charming as they were.

All summer, he worked on this delightful project. Then, travelling to Italy seemed necessary. Money was again scarce; Shelley had to feed so many people. He had in his charge Mary and the children, but also Claire and Byron's daughter, and quite often the Godwin family.

His new friend Leigh Hunt, his wife and five children had to be cared for too. Shelley had promised a £100 annuity to Peacock to help him to work in peace on his beautiful novels. He even paid the dowry for Charles Clairmont, who was not connected to him in any way, but who had met a charming but poor lady in France. As before, he had to borrow to pay these multiple demands. "You are," Godwin said, "a pureblood refrained from galloping by horseflies."

Fortunately, Mary helped him return to common sense and he forgave her, seeing her only through the Cythna of his poem. Mary, the worried housewife, did not like the frequent visitors though. Peacock came every night even without being invited and would drink a full bottle of wine by himself. She only wished Shelley would sell the house in Marlow they had bought too quickly in the first place. She could see he was suffering from the cold and longed for a milder climate, as in Italy:

> "My dearest love," she wrote to him in London, "may I ask you to be more transparent in your letters and tell me about your plans. Have you put the house up for sale? Did you tell Madocks what to say to possible buyers? Have you chosen Italy or the sea? Have you found some money for the travel? Also, could you do something for my father before we leave? Or else, would it be better if we now lived in a small house, on the beach, where we would spend far

less? You have not talked to Godwin about your projects in Italy yet, have you? If this is the case, may I ask you to do so, as I feel it is better to talk about these things, at least a few days before the departure.

"I have been out for the first time today. This house is terribly cold! I was freezing by the fireplace, but as soon as I was out, I felt the air warmer. I would like William to join me for my next walks. Could you please send an otter hat for him with the Monday car? It must be of the fashionable round shape; please do not forget to tell that it is for a boy, and it needs to be surrounded by a golden colour narrow ribbon which we can tighten when needed. I am overwhelmed with babies, I must say: Alba scratches and screams, William plays rolling himself in a shawl, while Miss Clara stares at the fire. Goodbye, my dearest, I cannot tell you how much I miss news of your health, your business and plan."

One of the complaints Mary had was about Alba's presence in their home; the neighbours were told that she was the daughter of a lady from London and had been sent to the countryside because of her health. However, everybody could see Claire's maternal behaviour, and many attributed the child to Shelley. The previous accusations of promiscuity were spreading about the household and upset Mary.

One of the reasons she wished to leave for Italy was that she wanted to take the little girl to her father. Shelley could not wait to leave too. He felt suffocated by the walls of resistance that family, friendship and business duties seem to impose on him, gently but methodically. It was as if small, seemingly casual yet treacherous waves of everyday life were chipping away at his inner strength.

In England, where the highest magistrate had taken away his civil rights as a father, he felt subjected to pillory. It seemed to him that in escaping from his own country, he could become once more an aerial and free spirit, and that abroad, his life would be like a blank page, where he could create a new life, just like a poem.

When the date of departure was agreed, Mary asked for the children to be baptised. She thought that for future happiness, it was better to start life again, but this time, according to some traditional rules.

Shelley agreed, and on the same day, Byron's daughter was baptised too and named Clara Allegra.

26
QUEEN OF MARBLE AND OF MUD

The clear sky of Italy is a trustworthy sky without any clouds. Once again, the three travelled by coach towards the country of both oblivion and sunshine; the company of the children and maids barely slowed down the vehicle's rapid, whimsical movements.

From Mont-Cenis, they reached Milan, where they had their first stop. They asked for news from Byron to whom Shelley had already written about the arrival of his daughter. In Milan, he stayed all day in the cathedral reading *The Inferno* and *The Purgatorio*. He liked the three giant, gothic windows which shed a religious light on the choir of Duomo. Churches did not inspire horror in him anymore; after having suffered so much misery, he found comfort in an environment that matched his feelings, an environment worthy of human passions. With Dante, and in this symphony of dark and warm colours, Catholicism no longer appeared to him as a mere invention of some usurpers.

They finally received Byron's reply to Shelley's letter. He did not want to see Claire and would leave on the spot any place that she came near. As for the little girl, he agreed to care for her, but only if he could be the sole carer in charge.

Shelley, finding these conditions quite harsh, tried to obtain some concessions. However, Byron who had initially refused to deal with Claire's squabbles ever again, totally rejected any changes to his offer. A Venetian man they had met in Milan said that the English Milord was enjoying a decadent life in Venice, and even had his own harem. This was certainly worrying for the future education of Allegra. Shelley recommended to Claire to simply forget about any possible help from Byron, and not entrust the child to him. As always, he would be responsible of all the costs involved. However, Claire was arrogant. Proud of Allegra's birth, she wanted the advantages for her daughter. She trusted Elise, the Swiss nanny who was caring for the little girl and so decided to send both of them to Venice. Despite the kind warnings from Shelley, the little girl was handed over to her father.

* * *

Soon, some alarming news about Allegra disturbed Claire. Byron had kept the child only a few weeks. First proud of her beauty, he let the Venetians admire and caress the child on the piazza. However, he became bored by this monotonous play and decided to entrust the child to the wife of the British consul in Venice, Mrs Hoppner.

Who was Mrs Hoppner? How would she treat an estranged child? Elise said that she was a good person.

However, Claire started to regret her decision. For one year, she had lived constantly with her daughter; she adored her; Allegra was the only being on Earth she could refer to as hers, since her family had rejected her, and her lover decided never to see her again.

Shelley realised her sadness and offered to go with her to Venice. Mary agreed, despite her distaste imagining the two of them travelling together. A servant named Paolo, an energetic and resourceful man, joined them as a courier.

In order not to upset Byron, who had previously forbidden Claire to come to any city he was in, they decided to stop in Padua, where they waited for the result of Shelley's diplomacy. However, Claire could not resist, feeling so close to Allegra. She thought to manage to see her daughter, while hidden. And so, with Shelley, she took a gondola down the Brenta. They reach the lagoon in the evening. As they crossed over in stormy weather, Venice's lights sparkled in a confusion beneath a curtain of rain.

The next morning, they went to the Hoppners, where they were received politely and with goodwill. Mrs Hoppner immediately sent someone to collect Elisa and the child.

Allegra had already gowned a lot. Albeit much paler and less lively, she was as beautiful as ever.

Then, they talked at length about Byron. Indeed, the Hoppners, respected couple with conventional ideas and morality, were nevertheless interested by all these intrigues. Despite being somewhat humanised by the unconventional Venetian life, the Hoppners shook their heads while telling the following:

On the third day following his arrival, Byron had obtained, as he liked to tell, both a gondola and a mistress. The mistress was named Marianne Segati, and she was the wife of the sheet merchant of Venice who initially rented a room to the poet. It was a reckless affair; sheets were not selling well. The woman was twenty-two, had delightful black eyes and a superb voice. Although from the middle-class, she was welcomed by the Venetian aristocracy, who liked listening to her singing. That she would fall for the foreign nobleman, who was handsome, generous and a genius, was as natural and inevitable as the simplest chemical reaction. As for the merchant of Venice, Byron was easy with money and in any case a wife's lover was tolerated in the city.

Mrs Hoppner, a petite, gentle woman with clever eyes, told this story with an air of sadness mixed with an eagerness that honest women generally have when they talk about vice. Her husband, with great caution, added that there was more. People were saying that the English lord had somewhere in town a hidden home where a single muse was not enough. Nine sisters gathered there. A whole legend had been created: English people related his story to Nero or even to Elagabalus. People were in awe, and under their carnival masks, a band of women used to gather around Byron.

These reports did not reassure Claire. She asked what she should do; the consul advised her to leave and avoid at any cost Byron being informed of her presence, because he frequently mentioned his great concern about ever meeting her again.

At 3 pm, Shelley went to meet Byron at the Palace Mocenigo. He was welcomed with grandeur. Shelley was probably the only human being Byron felt comfortable speaking with as an equal. Following the objective explanation of the purpose of their voyage, about Claire's desire to see her child, Byron remained calm and quite reasonable. He said that he understood clearly Claire's dilemma; however, he could not reasonably send the child back to her because of the Venetians, who had already accused him of having a capricious nature. They would conclude that he had become bored of the child; however, he would keep thinking through and try to find a way to reconcile everything. Then, he proposed a walk to the Lido.

The gondola took them across the lagoon. Horses were waiting on the half-submerged long beach, sown sparingly with thistles and algae. Shelley loved these deserted sands, galloping through the waves was just wonderful. His pleasure was spoiled by only one idea: that Claire anxiously waited for him.

Byron talked about the stupid attitude of the English gentry about him. Those who came to Venice were curious and sought him out. Some even paid his servants for the chance to look at his bed. Then, he started to talk about Shelley's hardship and rejection with many friendly arguments. "If I had been in England, I would have done anything possible to help you get your children back." Then, he developed and generalised the arguments about the nastiness of human beings, which he defined as unlimited:

"Human beings hate each other… Hoping and wishing something different is simply being a visionary."

"Why?" Shelley said. "You seem to accept the fact that humankind puts up with its basic instincts without being able to control them… My beliefs are rather different; I believe that our will can create our virtue… That nastiness is natural does not mean it is invincible."

Byron pointed out the patrician city: the sunset was rendering the sky dark purple and gold in fusion: "Let's go back to the gondola," he said. "I want to show you something."

After gliding across the lagoon for a few minutes, he started to speak:

"Look at the west side and listen. Don't you hear the clanging of the bell?"

Then Shelley saw, on a tiny isle, a building made of bricks, shapeless, nearly window-less and with a high tower in which a black bell was swinging against a vermilion sky. One would have said that the sound of distant cries mixed with the noise of the oars. "That is the mad house, said Byron. "Every night, when crossing the lagoon at this precise time, I listen to the bell calling the madmen for prayer."

"Probably to thank the creator for his goodness towards the madmen?"

"You will never change, Shelley!" Byron said, eagerly. "An infidel and a blasphemer!... And you cannot swim? Be aware of providence!... You were just talking about fighting our basic instincts?... Don't you think that this vista is reflecting our life? Our conscience is the bell that calls us towards virtue… And like these madmen, we obey, without knowing why. The sun sets, the bell stops, and then death comes."

He looked out towards Venice, which had become pinkish grey in the crepuscular light.

"Byron, we…" Shelley said, "we die young… on my father's and my mother's side… this does not bother me. However, I want to enjoy my youth as much as I can."

* * *

The next day, Shelley was surprised to find Byron quite reasonable. He agreed to leave for two months, at the disposal of Shelley and Claire, one of his villas near Venice, on the way to Este, and to authorise Allegra to stay with them. Shelley could not but accept such a generous proposal and wrote on the spot to Mary for her to come and join them. He wrote:

"I had to take the decision on my own; I believe that it was the best option, and you should, my lovely Mary, come and reprimand me if you feel that I was wrong, but kiss me if I am right. In my view, I do not know anymore, but future events will prove it either way. In any case, here, we will not have to bother to introduce ourselves, and you will meet Mrs Hoppner, who is simply delightful, as gentle as an angel, yet so wise. She could even be another Mary; however, she is not as perfect as you. Her eyes are simply a reflection of yours, when you know and like people… Please kiss for me the eyes of our darlings. Do not leave William to forget me another time. Clara, I know, is too little to remember me."

While travelling, Mary encountered some difficulties; she was detained in Florence with lengthy passport issues; Clara was teething and sickened with the heat and changes in her breastfeeding. When they arrived at Este, she became very ill.

She remained feverish for fourteen days. As the doctor from Este appeared quite ignorant, Shelley and Mary decided to take the child to Venice to consult a better one.

In Fusina, they were arrested by Austrian customs and denied passage across the lagoon. Shelley ignored the interdiction and pushed past with uncharacteristic aggression, hurrying everyone into a gondola. Little Ca suffered from strange convulsions affecting her eyes and mouth. She seemed unconscious most of the time. At the hotel, her symptoms worsened. There, a doctor said there was no hope. Sadly, the child died within the hour, quietly, seemingly not suffering.

Mary found herself in the inn's lobby, unknown to anyone, her dead child in her arms. Mrs Hoppner came and took her back to her home. The next day, Shelley stood in a gondola which sailed the tiny corpse to the Lido while Mary kept in check her terrible sadness. It was one of Godwin's principles that only weak and cowardly individuals show their sadness, and that really, grief does not last as long when one does not wallow in it, even secretly as a kind of cruel vanity to suffer. His daughter shared this belief. The next day following the burial, she wrote in her journal:

"Read the fourth canto of *Childe Harold Pilgrimage*. It is raining. Went to the Doges Palace, Ponte dei Sospiri, etc… At the academy with Mr and Mrs Hoppner, to see some fine painting. Visit to Lord Byron. There I met Fornarina."

* * *

Fornarina was Byron's new mistress. She was a girl with a mixture of wild and common looks:

> "You shall see how beautiful she is," Byron said to Shelley. "Big black eyes and the body of a Juno; wavy hair which sparkles with moonlight: one of those women who would go to hell for love. I love this kind of animal, as I would have preferred Medea to any other woman in the world."

This pretty baker was indeed a strange being, wild and indomitable. She was so ferocious that the servants feared her, even Tita, Byron's giant gondolier. Jealous, insufferable, false like a demon, and perfectly ridiculous when she replaced her beautiful shawl with elegant dresses and feather hats, which Byron used to throw on the fire. However, each time she bought new ones. However, he tolerated her madness, because she amused him. He loved her vivacity, her Venetian accent and her fury. This unsophisticated, animal-like soul relaxed him more than any spiritual work. Because of her, his poetry flowed abundantly and with ease, driven by a kind of uncontrollable force, a rage comparable to the ocean or even to a loving woman.

This admirable brute could only displease the Shelleys, who were civilisation itself. They exchanged sad looks during their few days in Venice. Shelley got closer to the real life of Byron and blamed him for it. The poet used for his debauchery women that the gondoliers collected in the streets, and then, disgusted with himself, claimed that being human was despicable. His supposed cynical nature appeared to Shelley as an elegant mask for his philandering.

Finally, the Shelleys went back to Este, sad to be going back without their little girl. However, there was joy in the house. In the garden, a path topped by vines on an espalier led to a charming lodge, which became a favourite retreat for the poet. From there, one could see Este's old castle and then, just like a green sea, the Lombardy plain, where beautiful villas resembling islands bathed in hazy air: far away, solitary Padua, and then Venice where gilded domes and campaniles shone together under a sapphire-blue sky.

Shelley was working again; he had started *Prometheus Unbound,* a lyrical drama inspired by the Book of Job; he tried to capture, through verses as light as wing strokes, the melancholic beauty of the autumnal light. However, no sooner had the intoxicating excitement of working faded away, he felt once more forgotten and isolated. It seemed to him that misery stood at the helm of the frail bark which sailed his group of exiles towards a foreign country beneath an alien sky.

27
THE ROMAN CEMETERY

After a month, they had to leave Byron's house and leave Allegra back with her father. The winter rain inspired Shelley to leave for the south. To be happy, he needed warmth and sympathy; unknown climates and cities tempted his melancholy.

The road to Rome snaked around reddish vineyards. One could see teams of milky white oxen of Virgilian beauty. They crossed Ferrara, then Bologna, where they saw so many churches, statues and paintings that they all felt their respective brains metamorphosed into an architect's portfolio or even a shop with printed etchings or books. Then, through the romantic towns, Rimini, Spoleto and Terni, the group reached the countryside of Rome where they found perfect solitude, both charming and sublime. At their arrival in the city, just above, a giant sparrowhawk glided in the sky.

In Rome, they were all moved by the majestic sadness of the ruins. Shelley was in awe of the English cemetery, close to the Pyramid of Caius Cestius, the most beautiful tomb, imbued with solemnity, he had ever seen. The wind was making the leaves sing just above the sepulchres of the children and women. It was a place where one could only wish to rest.

After three weeks of travelling, the group finally arrived in Naples, where they rented a house overlooking the blue bay, permanently similar yet constantly different. Night and day, one could see the smoke above Vesuvio with the sea reflecting its flames and shadow. The climate was similar to an English spring, though lacking the continuous crescendo of softness that characterises temperate climates. They went to Pompei, Salerno, Paestum: beautiful sights, which left only faint and confused impressions, like a half-forgotten dream. Despite all this beauty, they were not happy, sadness remained.

Neither of them knew anyone. The isolation of the little group has taken its toll. Under such beautiful sun, they remembered with nostalgia Richmond, Marlow, even London. What could these mountains, under such a beautiful blue sky, could possibly mean without any friends? Socialising is the alpha and omega of human existence; the surrounding landscape, so real, and as beautiful as it was, could just vanish into thin air, when compared with familiar decorum, perhaps mediocre, yet vividly coloured by intimate memory.

In the street, they looked with envy at the poor people, who were greeted by other poor people. Shelley, who had always felt too much for humankind, did not understand why he felt lonely even when surrounded by people. Mary was mostly suffering from being everywhere considered as a foreigner. She was again pregnant too and she could not stand Claire anymore; besides, she had major domestic issues. Paolo, her Italian butler, had been having an affair with the Swiss nanny. Mary insisted he should marry her, and when the rascal finally agreed, he left with his new wife, threatening revenge. Then, Claire became sick with a strange illness which Mary did not understand.

Disappointed, and tired of Naples, they decided to go back to Rome. They were animated by the perpetual need for change, like sick people desperately seeking a cooler place to soothe a fever. Sadly, the spring heat did not agree with William. The doctor recommended to quickly move up to the North. They were about to leave when William was struck by a violent bout of dysentery.

For sixty hours, Shelley did not let go of the little boy's hand. He was getting closer to him day by day. William was a bright boy, very affectionate and sensitive. He had silky blond hair, clear skin, and lively clever blue eyes. When the boy slept, the Italian women used to come on tiptoe to admire him. Even when he was in his death throes, the doctor still hoped to save him. He lived three more days, but then, at midday, under a fine sun, William died.

They buried William in the English cemetery, the solitude of which Shelley had previously found so charming. The wind was still singing among the leaves above. Close to a tomb from antiquity, surrounded by flowers and grass bathed in sunlight, Shelley witnessed the disappearance of his son.

Fanny… Harriet… little Clara… William… he had a strong feeling of being surrounded by a foul and pestilential air which infected one after another of his loved ones.

* * *

The gods seem to amuse themselves in hitting the young couple hard. So far, Mary and Shelley had withstood their hardship with bravery. However, this time, Mary simply gave up the struggle.

Shelley sent her to a beautiful villa in the countryside. However, she was not interested in anything. She only thought about William's little steps on Naples' beach, about his beautiful and naïve looks, which only love, amazement and pleasure can express. Motionless, her eyes fixed into the distance in a kind of torpor, she left her silence only to worry about the Roman tomb; she wanted white marble and flowers on her son's sepulchre.

Godwin was informed about her melancholic mood. He reprimanded her for it. Exhibiting such trivial pain only diminished her character, he thought; she was putting herself at the same level of other women. What was she lacking? She had the man of her choice and the financial means to be helpful to humanity. He wrote:

> You have lost one child, and so everything good in this world, the issues which require your goodwill, all of

these have become nothing in your eyes only because one three years old child has died.

Even Shelley complained, ever gently though:

"My dearest Mary, where have you gone, leaving me all alone in this gloomy world? Your shape is here, always charming, but you, you have fled and taken the path of solitude leading to sadness' darkest place…"

As for him, there were still aerial retreats where he could escape to and, from which the dark drama of his life revealed itself so absurd. There, he was finishing his *Prometheus*, a new metaphor for the unique theme of his work: the struggle of the human mind within the material world. Jupiter became in his work a kind of Lord Castlereagh; the enchained titan was another Shelley, a victim remaining full of hope, fully confident that goodness will triumph against evil. The beautiful cloudless sky, the whirl of the warm western winds, everything was a reason for *Ode to the west wind*, the desperately optimistic song, no hardship had yet destroyed:

> Scatter, as from an unextinguish'd hearth
> Ashes and sparks, my words among mankind!
> Be through my lips to unawaken'd earth
> The trumpet of a prophecy! O Wind,
> If Winter comes, can Spring be far behind?

When Mary was about to give birth, they left for Florence to be close to a good doctor. The best cure was Florence intellectual atmosphere itself, a city where solitude does not have any bitterness. In Florence, one can live with Dante, sit down close to Savonarola, or even imagine Giotto passing by. In the churches, Brunelleschi and Donatello are still friendly rivals. The statues live in the street, with more familiarity than anywhere else. On the piazza, David, the winner, defies the imbecile Neptune and the awkward Hercules by Bandinelli. One suffers less not knowing the children passing by, in the face of those of Della Robbia.

Shelley enjoyed looking at the city from the hights of San Minato. The pink roofs drew precise shapes; the Arno, swelled by the recent rains, was rolling its yellow waters between the old houses, which, from afar, resembled a human crowd running towards the banks and bridges; in the distance, one could perceive the valley and, further away, bluish hills.

In this spirited ambience, Mary, pregnant, recovered some zest for life. At the family's lodging, in all simplicity, she was happy to talk with people of lower class. Besides, the delivery of her baby was easy and quick.

When she held her baby in her arms, Mary finally smiled. This was the first time since William's death. She named her son Percy-Florence.

28
ANY WIFE TO ANY HUSBAND

Everything in life happens as a succession of events. One friend brings another one. Mary and Percy, who had previously suffered so much from their solitude, found themselves, without looking for it, at the centre of a small, active and agreeable group of friends.

This miracle happened by chance. First, Shelley felt the pain on his side again. The winds from the Apennines, so harsh in Florence during the winter, were affecting him. The doctor recommended he should go and live in the nearby, more sheltered city of Pisa.

Tom Medwin, one of his cousins, came to meet him. Tom used to be an officer in the Indian army. Newly interested in literature, he decided to try and find the only literate person in the family. He was boring yet, a good person. Furthermore, he introduced the Shelleys to a charming couple, the Williams.

Edward Williams had been, like Tom Medwin, an officer in the 8th Dragoon Guards. He was said to have resigned because of his health. He was a sincere man, simple, without any pretension, and furthermore interested in everything. The Shelleys liked him a lot. His wife appeared delightful too: pretty, with refined manners and an excellent musician. A serious and profound friendship quickly developed between the two families. The Shelleys finally found themselves living the kind of life with spontaneous visits, delicate compliments, and trust, which renders real friendships so charming.

Once a group is created, isolated individuals join. An Irish man came, Count Taaffe, a Greek man, the Prince Mavrocordato, and an extraordinary Italian priest, Professor Pacchiani, known as the Devil of Pisa because of his diabolical and piercing look of a Venetian inquisitor: he was an abbot without a religion, a professor without a chair, a great womaniser, a lover of painting, an antiquarian, a connoisseur and an international matchmaker. He was the man who could always find a palazzo available to rent, which would always benefit both the tenant and the owner, a man to recommend an Italian teacher and willing to share the costs of the lessons, the man who discreetly gives the name of a dealer willing to sell an Andrea Del Sarto.

Making himself at home the moment he entered, Pacchiani named Mary and her friend Jane *La Bella Inglese* and amused them with intimate stories about the Pisa aristocracy, whom he knew both as a friend and a confessor.

* * *

One of his stories vividly affected Shelley. Count Viviani, one of the most important men in the city, had recently got married for the second time, to a woman much younger than him; he had two charming daughters from his first marriage. The new countess, jealous of the beauty of the young girls, had managed to get her husband to send them away and isolate them in two different convents in Pisa, until someone agreed to marry them without a dowry. The professor, who had known the little countesses since their childhood, enthusiastically described their beauty and spirit. Emilia, the older, was even a genius.

"*Poverina!*" Pacchiani said. "She is there just like a bird in a cage. She is watching her youth passing by without any purpose: she, who was made for love. Yesterday, she was talking while watering the few flowers in her cell: "Yes," she said to them, "you were born to vegetate; however, us, spirited beings, we are made to be active and not wither immobile in one place…

He then said: "Sant Anna's Convent is a dreadful place indeed. At this very moment, the inmates are shivering from cold with only one tiny recipient of ashes to warm up. You would have so much pity for them."

Shelley's knight-errant feelings came back. They had been dormant during the past few years of married life. He asked plenty of questions, then demonstrated so much outrage about the old Count and such passionate interest for the young victim that Pacchiani, who could not resist the delightful opportunity to intercede knowing the supreme sensuality of the elder daughter, proposed taking Shelley to Sant Anna's Convent.

It was indeed a miserable building; the visitors crossed the gates, which were in ruins. The abbot called for Emilia. Soon Mephistopheles came back with Marguerite. Pacchiani had not exaggerated the young girl's beauty; her black hair was simply tied, like a Greek muse; her perfect profile resembled the work of a sculptor; her pallid tone made her seem half asleep, and made her voluptuous eyes sparkle even more. Italian eyes can sometimes surpass the renowned beauty of oriental sensuality.

As soon as she entered the sad parlour, Shelley fell for her. It was love, not physical desire, but rather an exquisite need to admire, to sacrifice oneself for the admired one. He had always retained in the background of his sensibility an image of perfect physical beauty associated with moral splendour, the mythical image of a charming and oppressed woman for whom he could become the knight, Andromeda and Perseus, or St George's princess: a myth that, in reality, lingered in the background, had driven him first to kidnap Harriet and then fall in love with Mary, because of her sadness. Unknown to him, a mixture of sensuality and pity confused his thoughts while inciting poetic elation and creativity.

For a long time, he had looked for the mystical lover. He had perceived Mary as a goddess-like woman. Probably and for the first time, the real Mary revealed herself, as the result of the dissipation of Shelley's mist, yet the real person mirrored with near perfection the previous idealised image. He realised soon that a couple had necessary features which could not be divine. Mary, mother and housekeeper, was in fact drier, more practical and pragmatic than the young heroic and gentle young woman from Skinner Street. What Shelley used to refer to as her clear, glass-like mind was becoming coldness; her jealousy sometimes appearing as vulgar petty-mindedness. But most importantly, he knew Mary so well now that it was impossible for him to link his reveries to that too precise and real image.

However, the young beautiful and mysterious woman incarnated the goddess because he knew nothing tangible about her. Finally, he was meeting the very being he had imagined since adolescence, fleeting and admirable. In the past, this imagined being evanesced each time he was about to reach her, with, instead, letting him with a real, flesh-and-blood woman who wounded his sensitivity.

On entering the parlour, Emilia had been talking to a bird in a cage. Shelley thought it was the most poetic talk in the world: "Poor birdy! You are dying of boredom! I feel so sorry for you! How much you suffer, listening to the flock of your fellow birds who are calling for you to leave for unknown countries with the wind! Like me, you must end your miserable destiny… O! I am just unable to free you!"

With ease, she improvised, in the Italian manner, some rhapsodies that did not lack in quantity or even power. Shelley found her formidable. He asked to see her again, to come with his wife and sister-in-law. She eagerly agreed.

In telling Mary about his encounter, he did not hesitate to let her know about his feeling. Both had read Plato, and Mary was aware of this kind of love, which is the very contemplation of supreme beauty. However, she would have preferred Shelley to contemplate a statue, or like Dante, to be unable to talk to his Beatrice ever. Yet, she agreed to go with him and see the captive beauty.

She recognised that Emilia was beautiful, like a Greek statue, and surprisingly eloquent. However, in her mind, she much preferred the prudish tact of the English ladies, rather than the emotional extravagance of the Italian ones. She found that Emilia spoke loudly; that her gestures, quite expressive, lacked grace, and that actually she was agreeable only when she was silent. However, she was careful to keep these impressions to herself, and demonstrated only care and friendship.

Claire, more sensitive, found her, like Shelley, quite appealing. When Mary brought to the captive cakes, books and a gold chain, Claire, who was penniless, offered what she could: English lessons, which Emilia accepted with joy. A frequent written communication started between the convent and Pisa; it was always "Dear Sister!...", "Adorable Mary!...", "Delicate Shelley!...", "*Caro fratello*", and even (the meaning should be understood here as mystical, of course) "*Adorato sposo*". Then, the "Dearest sister Mary" seemed to become colder. "However, your husband tells me that your apparent coldness is only ashes covering a very affectionate heart."

The truth is that dearest sister Mary was getting rather annoyed. Shelley was creating around Emilia one of his imaginary worlds in which he loved to escape; he was writing for her one long poem about love. He wanted it to be as mysterious as Dante's *Vita Nuova* or even Shakespeare's sonnets. He proclaimed in it his own doctrine about love:

"I have never been part of this important faction, which holds that each of the members must choose one mistress or friend, and forget the rest, however beautiful or wise. This is, however, the cult of these poor slaves who travel through the great path of the world towards their next home with the dead, and end up making the journey longer and harsher with a single enchained friend, or even a resentful enemy. True love, as opposed to gold or even to clay, does not diminish if divided. Love is like intelligence: more vivacious if contemplating more than one truth…

Narrow is the unloving heart or the mind focused only on one single thing."

Shelley portrayed Emilia with a pagan hymn singing the beauty of the captive:

> Warm fragrance seems to fall from her light dress
> And a loose hair, and where from heavy tress
> The air from its own speed had disentwined,
> The sweetness seems to satiate the faint wind
> To the glory of her divine personality,
> which pulsated in her limbs but also behind the clouds,
> In a quiet June sky,
> Where the moon shimmers beautifully and forever.
> Wife, sister, angel, pilot of the destiny
> So deprived from stars…
> Emilia, a vessel is rocking in the harbour…

Epipsychidion was to become the most passionate invitation to travel in a charming but unrealistic country:

> There, we will join to become one single being
> Our breaths will combine, our breasts will unite,
> Our arteries will beat the same rhythm,
> such a gentle ecstasy,
> We would die from it

Even if Mary, to reassure herself, repeated that these beautiful sentiments were aimed at Emilia's divine essence, and not at the pretty girl with black hair, it was difficult for her to see Shelley working with such exaltation. Fortunately, the work was becoming so demanding that he did not have much time to visit the heroine. And, while the platonic lover accumulated these floating images, Emilia had received a rather cynical proposition from the Count, her father.

The Count Viviani had found a husband who had agreed to marry her without any dowry; he asked her to make her mind up sooner rather than later. The husband was in fact quite attractive; he was a Biondi, living in a distant castle in the marsh land. She had never seen him and was not allowed to meet him before the wedding. This engagement in the Turkish fashion was indeed quite objectionable; however, could she hope for anything better? The king of the elves, married to the real Mary, would certainly not help her out of her captivity. If she was to marry this Biondi, maybe she would then find a way to a new life, a happier one? If the man displeased her, then she would be in a position to find someone else. There were probably some *cavalier servante* to be found even in the middle of the marshes.

Before finishing Epipsychidion, Shelley heard that Emilia was getting married.

* * *

Six months later, Mary wrote to a friend:

"Emilia married Biondi; it is said that she makes his and his mother's life terrible. The conclusion of our Italian-style friendship reminds me this nursery rhyme:

> 'As I was going down Cranbourne Lane,
> Cranbourne lane was dirty,
> And there I met a pretty maid
> Who dropped to me a curtsy
> I gave her cakes, I gave her wine,
> I gave her sugar-candy;
> But oh! The little naughty girl,
> She asked me for some brandy.'

"Replace the brandy with the money needed to buy it (not a small amount) and then you will understand the whole story behind Shelley's platonic love."

Shelley added in a letter:

"I cannot stand the sight of my poem anymore. The being I was singing for was aerial and not a goddess. I believe one is always in love with one thing or another: such an error.... and I confess that it is difficult for a spirit made of flesh and bone not to look for something that could be infinite in a mortal envelope."

29

THE CAVALIER SERVENTE

Following her departure from Venice, Claire received regular news about Allegra from the Hoppners. The little one was suffering from the Venetian cold. She had become quiet and serious, like an old lady. Mrs Hoppner suggested that the child should leave Venice. However, it was quite impossible to have a useful conversation with her father, who fell into a life of total debauchery.

Then, a few months passed without any news. Very anxious, Claire wrote more and more demanding letters; however, without any success. Oddly, the consul's wife remained silent, and Claire's letters went unanswered. Then, she heard that great changes had occurred in Byron's life. First, a major illness had confined him to bed. Hoppner, who stayed with him, told him that his love life no longer shocked the Venetians. Rather, it was a source of amusement to the gossips in *conversazioni* and in the parlours. It was said that sly girls had tricked him and were stealing all his money, and without his knowledge, mocked him in their dialect. Don Juan became furious and asked for all the 'priestesses' to leave Mocenigo palace with immediate effect.

During his convalescence and after a long absence, Byron could be seen again in Venice's parlours. There, he met the most beautiful woman of that era, the petite Countess Guiccioli, a charming young blonde girl of seventeen years, who had just got married to an old rather fogey baron. The foreigner found her rather well shaped. The first day, he gave her a secret note, which she skilfully concealed. It was a *rendezvous* proposition. She went. The great poet, young, handsome, a rich nobleman, declared his love for her. Surrounded by a thousand delights, she gave herself without any restraint.

A few days later, she had to leave for Ravenna with her husband, Count Guiccioli. Teresa asked Byron to come along. The pretty girl did not know that one can easily attract a man any time before… but after!

Byron did not like the idea of continuous fanciful love. He did not go and felt quite proud about his refusal. From Ravenna, she wrote to him that she was sick. Where love failed, pity won.

Don Juan left on the spot, still stopping on the way to Ferrara and other towns to admire local beauties. Even if he pretended not to be interested or even bored, he still happily welcomed encounters.

The poet was easily bored by clever ladies, such as Lady Byron or even Claire; he was so contemptuous of the female sex that he never expected intellectual company from any of his mistresses. The beautiful Venetian bakers or merchants were very different people and estranged to his status.

Countess Guiccioli had both, a kind and relaxing stupidity and the grace of a well-born lady: she managed to keep the permanent escapist close to her, without too much effort. Don Juan became her trusty and romantic caretaker. He wrote:

> "If I were to lose her, I would lose a being who has taken so much risk just for me and for whom I have so many reasons to love. I do not know really what I would do if she were dying. I know that I should shoot myself, and I hope I would do so."

When his victorious conquest had to leave Ravenna for Bologna, he followed her. He became the classical Cicisbeo, her cavalier servente:

> "But, I can't say that I don't feel the degradation and burden of it. Better to be an unskilful planter, an awkward settler or anything, than a flatterer of fiddlers and fan carrier for a woman… And now, I have become her *cavalier servente*! Oh my God! Such a strange feeling."

* * *

Claire heard about the whole story, that Byron had called Allegra to Bologna. The idea that her daughter was living at Byron's new mistress's home, a woman who certainly had no reason to love her and some to hate her, worried Claire very much indeed. She wrote a passionate letter, asking for the right to take Allegra back, to which Byron replied:

> "I am so much in disagreement with the education of adopted children in Shelley's household. I should think if I was sending my daughter to you, I was sending her to a hospital… rather, she should go to England, or into a convent. However, she will not leave me to die from hunger or of indigestion from green fruit, and to be educated believing that God does not exist."

Reading this letter, Claire resentfully wrote in her diary: "Letter from Lord Byron about green fruit and God", yet she cried a lot thinking Allegra, in a convent in the company of Italian nuns totally deprived of any notion of cleanliness or even, any love for children. She was simply horrified by this prospect. She wrote letters to Byron full of despair and aggressivity, close to being disrespectful.

Byron then wrote letters to Shelley complaining of Claire's attitude and to let him know that he did not wish to have any communication with her anymore.

> "I do not know," replied Shelley, "about what Claire has written. I have seen one or two letters; however, I found them so childish and silly. I even asked her not to send

them. She replied that she had written and sent others to you. It surprises me that you let yourself get upset with what Claire writes… It is quite normal that she wants to see her daughter, that her disappointment affects her, and that her sadness makes her write absurdities: that is quite normal really. Poor girl, she is sad and not well really, she should be treated with the utmost leniency. Individuals with weak character and minimal intellect should share with kings the absence of direct responsibility."

He needed some space to rise above the women's quarrels, which had become a disturbance, really. Mary was even more anxious. Godwin kept annoying her with money requests. Shelley decided not to respond anymore. He had given his father-in-law the equivalent of £5,000, without any positive result. In doing so, he had gained a kind of bitter wisdom, a painful understanding of Godwin's true nature with no positive attraction at all. Since the continuous, resentful letters from Godwin had started to affect Mary's breastfeeding, Shelley informed the philosopher that he would read his letters first, before Mary, and that he would not hesitate to delete those with financial demands:

"Mary has not and should not have any available money. If she had some, poor girl, she would give it all to you.

Such a father, I mean, a renown prodigy, should not lack other subjects to discuss with his daughter. You may think, since your letters will not benefit you anymore, of stopping all correspondence with Mary. I do not need to tell you this decision should be interpreted in one way only."

Ariel was becoming harsh.

Mary was worrying about her father, and Claire about her child. The women became exasperated by each other's company. Besides, their common admiration for the only man at home became rather an obstacle than a link within their shared suffering. Mary did everything to make Claire feel inadequate and inclined to leave. An old English lady found her a position as a governess in Florence; Claire finally left.

Shelley wrote long and kind letters to her. Even if they were innocent, he did not show them to Mary, and asked Claire not to mention them in her correspondence with her sister. However, he did not like at all this lack of openness he imposed on himself. Shelley conceived love as a space for shared ideas and actions, where explanations between lovers were pointless. The truth, in a pure wholly state, could be for some a deadly poison; and Mary could only stand it after strong dilution.

30
A SCANDALOUS LETTER

Venice 16 September

"My lord, you may be surprised, and rightly so, about my change of opinion regarding Shiloh. It is certainly not the one it was before. However, if I inform you about a terrible secret, may I expect you not to inform the Shelleys that you know, this for the respect of the poor lady but also for Mrs Hoppner and myself. I am certain that you will agree with this request and as such I shall now tell you the truth. For the benefit of Allegra, it is necessary that you are aware, because this will help you keep your resolution of not giving her back to her mother.

"Be aware that when the Shelleys were around, Claire became pregnant by Shelley himself. You may remember that she was constantly sick and cared for by a physician; I am not kind enough to believe that all the medicine she used to take was only to help her health. I also now understand why she wanted to stay on her own in Este, despite her known fear of robbers or even ghosts, rather than staying with the Shelleys.

"Whatever, they left for Naples, where, one night, Shelley was called for by Claire, said to be very sick. His wife, of course, found it rather strange that he was called for and not her; even though she did not know about the nature of their relationship, she had enough proof about Shelley's disinterest and about Claire's hatred for her. She remained calm, though only because Shelley asked her to.

"A midwife was called. The noble couple, who did not organise anything for the birth of this unfortunate being, gave money to the midwife and asked for the baby to be brought to the Pieta. The child was abandoned just thirty minutes after the birth. They had to pay a considerable amount to the doctor to buy his silence. During Claire's bedridden period, Mrs Shelley expressed some concerns yet, prevented from visiting her. These callous individuals, rather than thanking her for her concern, aggravated her feelings of hate. Their behaviour became odious, and Claire was doing everything possible to make her husband abandon her.

"Poor Mrs Shelley, even if she had some suspicions, she does not know anything. Since knowing would aggravate her misery, I really believe it is better she is not told. We have been made aware of this story by Elise; she has been staying here with a British lady, who spoke highly of her. She also told us that Claire, with no hesitation, told Mrs Shelley she wished to see her dead and even asked Shelley why he would stay with such a creature.

"I believe that after reading this story, you shall understand my bad feelings about Shelley. I recognise his talents, however, I cannot believe how such a man could be, as you rightly said once, 'madly against morality' and still be honourable. I know about the robber's code of honour; it is required for his self-interest. For Shelley, on the other hand, honour does not inspire any of his actions, albeit it is for his self-interest to appear respectable with the ideas he is trying to promulgate. I am afraid that this letter is a bit unclear and incoherent; however, I cannot resign myself to review it because of such a repugnant subject. I hope you will read it as it is and then make the effort to understand the facts… Goodbye, my dear Lord, your faithful servant, R. B. Hoppner."

Byron to Hoppner:

"My dear Hoppner, your letters and enclosed documents have safely arrived, even though a bit late, having missed the post. Shiloh's story is certainly true, even though Elise is here the mere witness for the prosecution. You may recall her great impatience to go back to them, but now she has left, she gossips about them. There are no doubts about the facts though. This is so like them. Be sure he shall listen to your advice. As always, your trusty friend."

31
LORD BYRON'S SILENCE

Shelley, invited by Byron to Ravenna to talk about one important matter. He found the traveller in good form. His face, which had looked tired from the Venetian debauchery of the past, was now glowing with good health. Guiccioli sovereignty prevented any other destructive relationships. Fletcher, the butler, looked better with more weight on too, like the shadow increases in proportion to the body that throws it.

The Palazzo Guiccioli was splendid: the way of life there was majestic. On the marble staircase, Shelley met animals of various species, all living together, as if at home. Eight enormous dogs, three monkeys, five cats, one eagle, one parrot and a falcon were all quarrelling just like a family. Ten horses were in the stables.

Byron welcomed him with attentive friendliness. The two friends passed the whole night reading their respective poems and discussing them at length. Shelley found Byron's new poems quite amazing. Yet, being in contact with the genius Byron made Shelley quite depressed. As opposed to Byron's forceful constructions, Shelley felt his own verses quite weak. He said to Byron that he trusted him perfectly able to write an epic poem that could be appreciated by the people of today and of the future as much as the *Iliad* had been by the ancient Greeks. However, Byron demonstrated only contempt for posterity; he was more interested in poetry for £1,000 guineas per poem.

Once again, the ascetic had to adapt to the way of life of the magnificent poet. Arise at midday, breakfast at two in the afternoon, and then work until six in the evening. Horse riding between six and eight, dinner, then discussion until six in the morning. Byron never elaborated about his poems and seemed rather more interested to discuss about life.

On the very first day, in a friendly way, he confided to Shelley about the gossip among the British expatriates in Italy, and, despite his promise to Hoppner not to discuss it, showed Shelley the letter which contained Elise's accusation. Byron said that, he had never believed this ridiculous story. However, Shelley became upset that the Hoppners had credited the gossip. He immediately wrote to his wife.

* * *

Shelley to Mary Shelley:

> Lord Byron told me about something that bothers me greatly, because it demonstrates such a desperate nastiness that I cannot comprehend. When I heard such a thing, my patience and my philosophy were both tested to such an extent, that I have had to restrain myself from escaping into some darkness where I would never have to look at a human

face ever again. Elise… [here he tells Mary about all the accusations written in Hoppner's letter]… Can you imagine how difficult and harsh it is for a weak and sensitive soul as mine to continue struggling in such diabolical human society? You should write Hoppner a letter, clearly denying the accusation and quoting the proof of your belief: only, of course, if you believe and can prove the fallaciousness of this accusation. I do not need to dictate to you what you must write, nor to inspire you with the necessary ardour to deny a calumny that only you can fully refute. Please, do send the letter to me here. I will then forward it to the Hoppners.

Mary Shelley to Shelley:

My dear Shelley, despite my unmeasurable distress, I am writing the enclosed letter. If the task cannot be too awful for you, could you copy it please; I just cannot. Please, do also copy your letter's paragraph with the mention of the accusation. I tried to write it down, but I have failed. I think that I would have rather died. I have enclosed Elise's letter too. On your side, enclose it with your letter if you wish. Yesterday, I wrote to you in a different state of mind from today. Oh, my dearest darling, I love you so much. Our common barque has been shaken so much by the storm; however, keep loving me as you have always done, and if God cares for my children, we should have enough strength to fight against our enemies...

Goodbye, my dearest darling, please be careful. All is well, despite everything. On my side, the shock is over. I despise defamation; however, it cannot remain unopposed. I thank Lord Byron sincerely for his goodwill and his refusal to give it any credibility.

Post scriptum: Do not think I was unwise to have even mentioned Claire's sickness in Naples. I believe it is positive to look at the facts objectively. They are as cunning as much as nasty. I have read again my letter in haste; however, I have expressed my feelings with my initial red-blooded reaction.

(Mary Shelley to Mrs Hoppner:)

After two long years of silence, I am writing to you even though I am sorry to have to write to you under such circumstances... I am writing to defend Shelley, my partner in life who I love and esteem above any other living being. I am writing about odious gossips; it is to you that I must write to you, who was once so kind, and to Mr Hoppner, as it was once so delightful for me to think that I owed you only gratitude.

It is now a very painful task.

Shelley is currently with Byron in Ravenna. I have received today a letter from him, which makes my hand shake so much so that I have difficulty even holding the quill… It is said that Claire is Shelley's mistress, and that… I just cannot write the following words. I am sending you an extract of Shelley's letter to me for you to see what I am unable to write down. I would prefer to die than write such a low statement, so nasty and untrue, such inconceivable, monstruous words.

However, the fact that you have believed them, that my dearest darling could have been slandered that way in your own mind, him, the most delicate and finest man, this very fact is very gruelling to accept. O! This is so much harder than any words can express. Could I tell you that my relationship with Shelley has never been in trouble? Love caused our first imprudence: a love, which, augmented by mutual respect, by perfect trust between each other, has continued growing and has no limit…

Those who know me well, always trust my words. Not so long ago, my father wrote to me that he had never heard me telling a lie. For you, who have so easily accepted such a lie, it may be easier to remain deaf and not listen to the truth. To you, and with everything on Earth and beyond that is sacred to me, I swear solemnly, I would die for if I was writing a sermon to tell about the lie; I swear against the life of my child, of my dearest, lovely child, that I know it is a lie, a whole lie.

Have I said enough to convince you, or are you still dubious in some way? Repair, please, I am asking you to repair the wrong you have done in placing your goodwill in such a revolting being as Elise. Please, can I ask you to write back to me that you shall now stop believing anything she gossips about us. You have been good to us; I shall never forget. Now, I am asking for justice. You must believe me. Be just and confess to me that you now trust my words.

Shelley showed this letter to Byron and asked him for the Hoppners' address. In reply, Byron asked him to trust him to personally send the letter. "I swore to the Hoppners," he said, "that I would not tell you about this vulgar gossiping about; as I have to admit to them that I did not keep my word. I must follow my words and polite rules. This is why I ask you to allow me to give by hand this letter. Furthermore, my arguments should give it more weight."

Shelley eagerly agreed and gave the letter to his friend. Mary never received any response.[1]

* * *

Byron wished to address with Shelley the important issue of Allegra, and what should happen to her when he should leave Ravenna. The Countess Guiccioli wanted to leave for Switzerland; Byron, who preferred Tuscany, asked Shelley to write to her about the pleasurable and gentle life in Pisa and Florence, to persuade the countess to accept moving there.

Shelley had not met his friend's mistress yet. However, he did not hesitate to write the requested letter, he was so used intervening in person in his friend's issues. The letter ended up so persuasive that it won. In an instant, it was decided that both Byron and his companion would leave to join the Shelleys in Pisa. As for Allegra, Byron agreed to bring her with them, since Claire was not in Pisa anymore.

Before leaving Ravenna, Shelley went to see the child in the convent of Bagna-Cavallo. He found her taller, still with very delicate features, yet quite pale. Her beautiful black hair fell in heavy curls on her delicate shoulders. Among her companions, she appeared different, as if from a more delicate and noble race. A kind of serious, contemplative attention had replaced her previous liveliness.

Her initial shyness dissipated, to be replaced by leniency following the gift from Shelley of a gold chain brought from Ravenna especially for her. She invited him to follow her into the garden. There she ran and skipped so fast that it became hard for him to follow. Then, she showed him her small bed and unique chair. He asked her what he should say to her mother:

> *"Che mi manda un baccio e un bel vestituro."*
> *"E come voi il vestituro sia fatto?"*
> *"Tutte di seta e d'oro."*

And to her father:

> *"Che venga farmi un visitino e che porta seco la mammina."* [2]

It was a difficult message to send to her noble father.

Her main character trait seemed to be vanity. She was not very educated; however, she knew many prayers by heart, spoke about paradise, dreamt about it and knew a great deal about the names of saints. Byron was pleased to learn about this type of education.

32
MIRANDA

The expected arrival of the noble tourist excited the small circle of friends in Pisa with the gratifying agitation always created by visiting aristocrats. Mary, under Shelley's order, had rented the most beautiful house in the city: the Lanfranchi palace. With the help of their friends, the Williamses, she had made this old building fit to properly welcome Lord Byron. Soon, Lady Guiccioli arrived first, accompanied by her father, Count Gamba. The Shelleys welcomed her. This pretty and petite Italian woman, romantic and childlike, surprised and delighted them. "She is a charming lady," Shelley said and added "if I understand well human nature and my friend Byron, she shall soon regret her silly carelessness."

Then, Don Juan revealed himself. All Pisa was at the window to catch a glimpse of the English devil and his menagerie. The parade was worth watching: five coaches, seven servants, nine horses; dogs, monkeys, peacocks and wading birds followed. The Shelleys were worried about the impression their palace would make; however, it pleased the newcomers. Byron said that he liked this old home from the Dark Ages. However, the palace was from the Renaissance

16th century. The lord often mixed styles and history. The dark and humid cellars appeared to him quite romantic. He named it the underground dungeon, asked for cushions to furnish it and decided to make the cellar his bedroom.

From his arrival, he became the mondain hub of attraction for the Pisa group. One paid a visit to Byron as a matter of curiosity or admiration, and to Shelley for sympathy. Shelley would rise early to read Goethe, Spinoza or Calderon; then he would leave for the pine woodlands, and in this nearly perfect solitude, work until the evening. On the other hand, Byron awoke at midday, had a light meal and then went to pay a visit to his mistress, returning at eleven in the evening to start working until two or three in the morning. Then, feverish and excited, he would retire to bed, sleep badly to then stay in bed all morning.

He attracted the whole English expatriate community. The most puritan of them could no longer be offended by an authentic lord who was able to bring to a foreign land such an example of English vanities. Was the pleasure Byron took to be scandalous a sign of the most orthodox sign of respect? If indifference is an insult, on the contrary could an insult be a form of humility? Was it not obvious that he could not live without parlours and clubs to visit, women to charm, dinners to organise? Much leniency was given. However, when the same was asked for

Shelley, there was a stubborn resistance. In society, Shelley appeared quite bored. One could detect his preference for the spirit rather than the words when it came to ethics, that he believed more in redemption than in the original sin. His belief in the perfectibility of humankind could not be forgiven because it would impose the courage. Frivolity, which can smell it from afar, has only one purpose, to destroy it; the most distinguished ladies treated Shelley with suspicion.

As for him, he could not care less, he far preferred the fresh night air to the smoky air of a cardroom. However, Mary wished so much to be invited. A lady with the name of Mrs Beckett was organising balls; "being," said Byron, "afflicted with a litter of seven girls, all of them of an age where girls need to dance to survive." It became a fixation for Mary to get an invitation to one of Mrs Beckett's balls. "Everybody is going," she said. Shelley, feeling disappointed, gazed towards the sky: "Everybody! Who is this mythical monster? Have you ever seen it, Mary?"

To please and meet "everybody", she even tried to go to a service with the Anglican pastor. However, he started to preach against atheists, while fixing her with a look of such intensity, that despite her conformist fervour, she felt that, because of her wifely dignity and duties, she could not ever go back.

These worries, dinners and balls of the high society were all perceived by Shelley as incredibly trivial. At twenty years old, frivolity had appeared to him like a crime; there, he judged it appalling and quite contemptible, which was even worse. To escape the reprimands and regrets which he found so ridiculous, he took refuge at the Williamses. There, he seemed to find the harmony and gentle atmosphere that was so essential for him. Edward Williams was cheerful, generous, without any kind of pettiness. As for Jane, her grace, her gentleness, the elegance of her movements, her soothing voice, all combined to make her a lovely and calming being, comparable to a beautiful garden. It is possible that she would not have been so attractive to Shelley when he was twenty and dreaming of a strong and fiery virgin, but now, he was looking for oversight rather than strength from a woman.

When she sang, Shelley was transported far away from his past tragedies and from the mundane reality of his couple life. As before, after having been hurt by Harriet, and with an endless pleasure he had looked at Mary's full of promise beauty; now, he found Mary flawed and most of the time complaining of something or another. He enjoyed contemplating Jane as a mortal image of Antigone, whom he had probably loved before, in a previous life.

However, he did not think as before. He did not think of breaking up everything to then build something new, to leave Mary and run away with Jane. Also, she was married to a good man he wanted to stay friends with. Mary was a sad but good woman; he had to manage her hypersensitivity. He loved Jane, but his feeling was ethereal, with no hope and almost without desire.

With delight, Miranda played this chivalrous game skilfully, and sometimes caressed Shelley's forehead while trying to heal his sad passion with gentle and magical vibrations. Jane and Edward were potentially a marvellous source of happiness and friendship, where a tired poet who had suffered so much was welcome to cool his feverish state. They could be Ferdinand and Miranda, a beautiful, princely couple, and Shelley their trusty Ariel. Around the happy lovers, he was the pure and enthralled spirit.

* * *

The Williamses often talked about one of their friends, Trelawny, a special man, a corsair, a pirate, who, at nineteen years old, had already sailed around the world. Trelawny wanted so much to join them all in Pisa. He wrote many times: "If I come, will I meet Shelley? Also, will I meet Byron? Is it possible to get close to both?"

Edward Williams, as their new acquaintance, had dispossessed the two poets of the prestige of being either mysterious or difficult. He replied with a touch of impatience: "Certainly, you shall meet them both. Shelley is a man of the simplest world... As for Byron, all shall depend on you."

Trelawny arrived late one evening and went first to visit his friends, the Williamses; As all three were engaged in an animated discussion, he glimpsed though the half-opened door, two sparkling dark eyes fixed on him; Jane stood up and said, smiling: "Come in, Shelley, our friend Trelawny has just arrived."

Shy and now blushing, Shelley entered and cordially shook the mariner's hands. Trelawny looked at him, quite surprised. He could not comprehend that those feminine features were those of the rebellious prodigy, despised in England, considered as a monster and deprived of his parental rights by the Lord Chancellor.

As for Shelley, he instantly admired the wild and self-assured face, the corsair's dark moustache and his beautiful half-Arabic features. Both were so amazed that neither of them could speak. To break this embarrassing silence, Jane asked Shelley about the book he was holding.

> "El *Magico Prodigioso*, by Calderon;
> I am translating a few pages."
> "Please, read them to us."

And then, Shelley, as if liberated from the awkwardness of social convention, escaped with joy and immediately translated aloud with such perfection and ease that Trelawny's doubts totally vanished.

At the end of the reading, Trelawny raised his head and surprised not to see the reader, asked: "But where has he gone?"

"Who?" Jane said. "Shelley? He just comes and goes, like a spirit and nobody knows where or how."

The next day, Shelley himself invited Trelawny to accompany him to Byron's home. There, the decorum was quite different: marble hall, grand stairs, servants and hostile dogs. Trelawny, like everybody, saw in the person of Byron another genius; however, he found conversation with the great man surprisingly trifling. It was like he was playing a part, an old-fashioned one, that of a Regency rake; he talked about actors, drinkers or even boxers' stories and how he swam the Hellespont. The challenge was very dear to him.

At three, the horses were ready; following a long ride, they stopped at a small inn. A servant brought some pistols; and behind the house, a stick was put in the ground, a coin fixed in a slit at the top. Byron, Shelley and Trelawny fired one after the other; Trelawny was happy to see that despite his feminine appearance, Shelley used the pistol like a man.

On the way back, they talked about literature and the richness of some rhymes. Trelawny quoted as an example two verses of *Don Juan*, which attracted the attention of Byron, who from that moment rode by his side.

"So, be honest," he said. "You expected to find in me *Timon of Athens* or even *Timour The Tartar*, and you are quite surprised that in fact you found a gentleman, never serious and who makes fun of everything."

In a low voice, he then murmured: "The world is like a haystack people fight for…"

* * *

Then, Trelawny, Shelley and Mary all left. "Byron is so different from what one would expect," Trelawny told them. "He is not mysterious: he speaks very freely; he says things which should not be said. He seems jealous and quite instinctive, just like a woman, but probably more dangerous."

"Mary," Shelley said, "Trelawny has already unmasked Byron. How stupid we have been! How long this has taken us!"

"This is due," Mary said, "to the fact that Trelawny lives among the living while we are living with the dead."

33
THE DISCIPLES

The mariner who came especially to Pisa to admire the two great men found himself admired in return. It is also true that when he was not around, Byron used to say: "If at least we could teach him to wash his hands and not to lie, we could make him a gentleman." However, most of the time they treated him with great respect. Like all artists, Byron and Shelley created poetry to comfort themselves about their inability to live fully. The action man appeared to both men, creators of fiction, like a strange yet desirable phenomenon.

Shelley asked Trelawny regularly about nautical terms and their use, and would draw keels, sails and maritime maps on the Arno sand: "I have failed," he said, "I should have been a mariner."

"One cannot make a mariner from a man who does not smoke nor swear," Trelawny replied. Byron, an imaginary corsair, wished to learn from the real one about the habits of the profession and made a conscious effort to appear cynical and courageous in his words. Trelawny, who quickly understood his influence on the two great men, promised himself to uniquely serve Shelley.

"Do you know," he said to Byron one day, "that you could do so much good for Shelley, just by writing about him as you have already done for less talented people?" Byron looked upset and replied: "All professions have their secrets, Trelawny. If I praise one popular author, he shall in return pay me back the same amount, with capital and interest. However, Shelley is a bad investment... Who is reading Shelley? Anyway, if he were to stop writing his metaphysical essays, he would even not need me."

"Why do your friends treat him in such a cavalier way? When they meet him at your place, they do not even acknowledge his presence. He is as aristocratic and educated as you are. Are they scared of something?"

Byron smiled, shook his head and whispered mysteriously in Trelawny's ear: "Shelley is not a Christian."

"And your friends?"

"Ask them yourself."

"In my view," Trelawny said, "if ever I were to meet the devil himself, I should treat him as one of your friends."

Byron studied him closely to find out if he was serious. Then, pushing his horse towards Trelawny, he leaned in and told with a quiet voice suggesting together fear and respect: "The devil is an aristocrat."

* * *

Trelawny discussed at length his observations with the Williamses. The three of them were like the chorus of a tragedy. Nice people who know they cannot play the main role, find great pleasure in being critical of the protagonists.

"One might think," said Trelawny, "that Byron is jealous of Shelley. However, Byron's publisher must ensure police protection on the publication day of a new canto of *Childe Harold's Pilgrimage*, while Shelley knows only ten or so readers; Byron has the wealth, the nobility, beauty, glory, love…"

"Yes," said Edward Williams, "however, Byron is a slave to his mood and any imprudent woman. Shelley is not. In a nutshell, he would lie down in the Arno refusing to be taken away by the flow. His ideas are rigid; he has a doctrine. Byron cannot keep one for more than two hours. He knows this and cannot but regret this reality. And this can be heard when he gloats like a winner about Shelley's miseries."

"Byron," Jane added, "is a spoiled child… neither of them understands human society; Shelley loves humankind too much, Byron not enough."

"What is terrible," said Trelawny, "is that Shelley does not have any instinct or even understanding for civilised trivial conversation… the other day, when I was about to swim in the Arno, he told me that he regretted not knowing how to swim… 'Try, I told him on the spot… Just lie down on your back, and you will float'. He then took off his clothes and without any hesitation, jumped in. He went right down and remained there without moving at all, just like an eel in the silt… If I had not jumped in and rescued him, he would have simply drowned without any struggle whatsoever."

Jane sighed; she knew that Shelley had suicidal tendencies. He often said that most people he had once loved had died that way: "However, he does not seem unhappy really. No, he lives in his dreams. However, do you think that in real life he does not suffer from being unable to promulgate his ideas and his work without any readers, or even because of his flawed marriage? Death may seem to him an awakening following a nightmare."

"Shelley believes in an afterlife," Trelawny said. "Those who call him an atheist do not know him well. He has often told me that the previous century's French philosophy now appears to him literally false and even pernicious. In his mind, Diderot has been defeated by Plato and Dante. However, he still does not regret his position against the established orthodoxy… I asked him once: "Why are you saying that you are an atheist? This very statement prevents you from being listened to?" He replied: "It is a painted iconic evil to only scare the imbeciles".

And so, the group of friends discussed him probably without realising the root cause of their unanimous adulation for Shelley was his social failure. People seem to prefer those they can feel sorry for, rather than those they feel envious of. People find in one's undeserved failure, arguments to explain their own bad luck. A mixture of both admiration and pity is the best appeal for one's affection. Williams and Trelawny would have needed humility to like the brilliant Byron as much as they appreciated the poor Shelley.

While the group of disciples talked about the absent master, he worked in the pine woodland which bordered Pisa's outskirts. There, Shelley used as a natural shelter a huge tree, uprooted by the sea wind. He nested there just like a wild bird. From afar, his den could be identified by the presence of scattered pieces of paper covered with unfinished verses.

While daydreaming, he sometimes forgot about dinner or even about his own existence. Mary often had to go looking for him. Trelawny escorted her; he behaved as if he were the 'cavalier servant' of the abandoned lady and charmed her, like a pirate. This amused the noble woman she was. When tired, she would sit down at the entrance of the woodland. There, Trelawny left her to hunt for the poet. One day, when he found Shelley daydreaming, he did not risk interrupting him. To attract his attention, he gently made some dry pine needles crackle under his feet. He then took Aeschylus and Shakespeare, and then a piece of paper on which he had scribbled, "To Jane, with her guitar"; however, Trelawny could only decipher the first two lines: "Ariel to Miranda. Take this slave of music"

He called Shelley, who then turned his head and faintly said: "Hello! Come in". "So, this is your study, is it?"

"Yes, and these trees are my books. When one writes, the attention needs to be freely divided. At home, there is no possible solitude: one door shutting, a step, a ring, everything echoes in the mind to dissolve the visions."

"Here, you can listen to the river, to the birds."

"The river is flowing just like time; nature sounds are soothing. Only the human animal is discordant and bothers me… O! How difficult it is to understand why we are here, what a perpetual worry for ourselves and others!"

Thinking of Mary, worried and waiting at the edge of the forest, Trelawny interrupted Shelley. He got up, collected all the books and papers, put them in his pockets and hat, and then sighed still thinking: Poor Mary, she is unlucky, she cannot stand neither the solitude nor the society… A woman full of life linked to a half-dead man.

Shelley followed Trelawny, gliding like a spirit through the fields and forests.

On seeing Mary again, Shelley started to feel apologetic. However, even obviously worried, Mary retained a Godwin-like prudish composure which successfully hid any feelings.

Instead, she teased him: "What a silly goose you are, Percy! If I was thinking about something other than my book, it would be about the opera or the new dress from Florence I am waiting for, or even and most importantly, about the ivy crown for my hair, and not about you, my great canary! When I left home, my satin shoes had not yet arrived… Those are the important things for me.

However, there remained something persistently dissonant in Mary's cheerfulness.

34

I SHALL GO TO HER, BUT SHE SHALL NOT RETURN TO ME

II Sam, xii, 23

Byron, having promised to bring Allegra to Pisa, arrived without her. Claire, who had left Florence in the hope of being able to have a glimpse of her daughter, became very worried when she heard that her daughter had been left behind in the Bagna-Cavallo convent, a place her Italian friends described as sinister. The house was built in the swamps of Romagna, one of the unhealthiest climates. She was told that hygiene was ignored, the food was disgusting and heating unheard of. Claire could not see a fireplace without thinking of her daughter deprived of warmth.

Maternal suffering pushed this small, proud woman to a quite sublime renunciation. She wrote to Byron that she would accept not seeing Allegra anymore if he would agree to send her to a good English school. "I can no longer resist," she said, "an inexplicable and stressful feeling that I shall never see her again."

Byron did not reply. Some friends advised Claire to kidnap her daughter; however, Shelley asked her to be patient.

While agreeing about Byron's cruelty, he disagreed with any impulsive reaction: "Lord Byron is uncompromising, and you are at his mercy. Do remember, Claire, that you treated my previous advice with undeserved contempt, and now you regret it. This is my second Sibylline oracles. In case you are waiting for the third one, this would probably cost even more."

He tried to talk to Byron. But as soon as he heard the name Claire, Byron showed his impatience: "Oh!" he said, women cannot live without having arguments." Then, Shelley told him about the issues of hygiene in the convent, as it had been reported to Claire: "How can I know?" Byron replied. "I have never been." Then, when he was told about Claire's torments and concerns, he smiled like a satisfied demon.

When leaving, Shelley said to an old English friend: "I had to restrain myself from hitting him. I was furious and I was wrong. He cannot avoid being who he is, like this door is just a door." "Your matter-of-fact attitude is absurd, really," said the old gentleman. "Even if I were flogging this door, it would remain a door; however, if Byron were properly flogged, he would become as human as he is now inhuman. It is the weakness of his friends that allow him to be this insolent tyrant.

Hearing about the failure of Shelley's approach, Claire became so desperate that both Mary and Shelley felt it was impossible to leave her with strangers in Florence. Therefore, they invited her to join for their visit to the Williamses on the coast.

Shelley promised himself to make this holiday as happy as possible. With Williams and Trelawny, he ordered the building of a boat in Genoa by Captain Roberts, one of his friends. They had already baptised it *Don Juan*, in Byron's honour.

On his side, Byron had ordered an even bigger yacht, which he named the *Bolivar*. Shelley and Williams were already seeing themselves as the masters of the Mediterranean Sea. Their respective wives did not show the same enthusiasm though. While their husbands drew maps on the sand, they walked around, talking philosophy while picking violets along the way. "I hate this boat," Mary said. "O, me too," Jane replied. "However, whatever we would say, it would be useless anyway. Worse it could seven spoil their happiness."

To manage this project, they needed two houses situated on the coastline. Shelley and Williams searched in vain. Lord Byron, who initially wanted to acquire a palace, just gave up. It was impossible even to find any simple fishermen's cottage. Williams and his wife decided to have another try, and asked Claire to come with them, to distract her for a bit.

They had only been gone a few hours, when Lord Byron wrote to Shelley that he had just received bad news about Allegra. There was a typhoid epidemic in Romagna. The nuns had not taken any precautions. The child, already weak and tired, contracted the fever and died. "I do not feel," he added, "that I have any responsibility in that matter. However, I am certain of my intentions and feelings. Sometimes, one can think that doing this or that could have prevented a tragedy; however, each day and even each hour passing by are a testimony that these tragedies are inevitable. I suppose that Time will do its work: Death has done its own."

They went and visited him. He was even more pale, and quieter than usual.

Two days later, the Williamses and Claire returned from their travel. Shelley, concerned about Claire's inevitable agitation on learning about the misfortune, decided not to say anything prior to their departure. Williams had not found the two houses they were looking for; Casa Magni, a large, ruined building, unfurnished and with a large terrace overlooking the sea, became their only option.

Shelley, who wished at all costs to drive away Claire, decided to rent Casa Magni. The two couples would live together. Was it inconvenient? That did not matter. Was there any furniture? So, some furniture would be brought up from Pisa. At those times when his will was completely engaged, nothing was an obstacle: "I will go," he said, "until something stops me. However, nothing does ever stop me."

The customs and the mariners created some complications, but he resolved all of them, with a single fixed idea, that was not taking into account the external world. And within a few days, the two families were able to travel to the seaside.

* * *

Casa Magni, once a Jesuit convent, was a white house, almost surrounded by water and close to the forest. A terrace with arches overlooked the magnificent gulf of Spezia. The ground floor was uninhabitable, invaded by the sea as soon as it was high. Only paddles and fishing tools were left there. On the first floor, a large dining room opened to the Williamses' bedroom on one side, and on the other side, to the bedrooms of Shelley and of Mary and Claire.

It was not enough. On the first evening, they exchanged their feelings of discontent, while the waves crashed constantly against the rock with a mournful sound. The Williamses and Shelley meditated on Claire's misery. She, who was still ignorant about it, assumed their discomfort was about her presence in this tiny house. She said it and even offered to leave for Florence. The two couples protested: Jane murmured something to Mary, they both stood up and went to the Williamses' bedroom; then, Shelley followed. Claire stood up and drew close to the bedroom; she saw them huddled together in a corner in agitated conversation, which stopped as soon as they saw her. And then, without a single word pronounced by the others, she said: "Allegra is dead, isn't she?"

The next day, she wrote Byron a terrible letter, which he immediately sent back to Shelley together with his written complaints about Claire's harshness and that he, of course, would pay for their child's funeral and sepulchre. To which she replied, with some kind of dark irony, that she would leave it to him: she only asked for a beautiful miniature and one blonde curl. She said goodbye to her friends in Casa Magni and went back to Florence, to live among strangers who knew nothing about her past and would not bother her at night.

The noble lord decided to have his daughter buried in England, in Harrow church, and to place on the wall above her tomb a marble tablet with the words:

TO THE MEMORY OF ALLEGRA DAUGHTER
OF GEORGE GORDON LORD BYRON DIED
AT BAGNA-CAVALLO, THE 20TH of APRIL 1822
AGED FIVE YEARS AND SIX MONTHS.

I shall go to her, but she
shall not return to me
II Sam, xii, 23

However, Harrow's vicar and several members of the parish council found immoral to welcome in their church a child outside the wedlock, especially if the name of the father was to be inscribed. And so, Claire's daughter was buried outside the church, without any inscription.

Following Allegra's death, Lord Byron visited the convent at Bagna-Cavallo for the first time. His previous strong and negative feelings about it transformed into a romantic and sentimental impression. He found it a place where he could meditate on death and on himself.

"I shall go to her, but she shall not return to me." The second verse of Samuel was quite right.

35
THE REFUGE

For Shelley, Casa Magni was enchanting. He loved its wild solitude, the forest behind the house, the rocky and woody bay, and the humble villages of the fishermen.

Mary felt lost and unhappy, though. Pregnant again, she was sick and worried. She would have much preferred to live in a city, near a doctor. She disliked the coastal villages and their tough inhabitants, as much as the Tuscan charm had pleased her in the past. Furthermore, Jane Williams's presence, once delightful, just became annoying. The shared household proved difficult for the women. There were trivial disputes about servants or even the pans. Shelley was talking rather too much about Jane's perfection and was now writing serenades for her.

To any complaint from his wife, he responded with a constant good spirit. Slowly, gently, he would then caress her, trying to comfort her: "Poor Mary," he said, "it is a Tantalus punishment that a woman with such qualities, with such a pure soul, in reality, is unable to inspire sympathy."

He knew that he could not change her, that her physical state explained most of her weaknesses. He tried to support her with patience and affection. What she blamed him for was his total disregard for what other men usually felt desirable and worth fighting for. She admired him as much as the first day she had met him; only in him did she feel a vigour on which she could count. However, something undefinable prevented him using this vigorous power to benefit himself. It always seemed as if his own interest was foreign to him. His being was not, as it is for other people, limited by precise boundaries, it extended a sort of luminous halo that reached his friends and even people he did not know. As for worries, or even the conventions of human society, he continued to ignore them.

Every month, he used to leave for Livorno to collect his annuity. He would come back with a bag full of coins and empty it on the sitting room floor. Then, with the charcoal shovel, he skilfully gathered the *scudi* to build a kind of cake, which he then flattened carefully with his shoes. With the shovel, he then cut in two the newly formed cake. One half was for Mary, for the rent and the household. The other half was then cut in two: a quarter for Mary's personal spending and the other for Shelley. However, Mary knew very well what 'for Shelley' meant: it was for Godwin (despite all the talking), for Claire and the Hunts.

One day, Mary invited round some nosy English aristocrats, who were curious to meet the poet. Since Shelley was not yet back, they sat at the dinner table without him.

Suddenly, one of the women shouted: "Oh! My goodness!" Mary, turning around saw Shelley, totally naked, trying to hide behind the servant.

"Percy!" she said, "how dare you?"

It was unwise from her. Indeed, Shelley, feeling wrongly accused, abandoned his refuge and came close to the table to defend himself. The women hid and covered their face with their hands. In reality, he was still charming, even with his hair entangled with kelp and his frail body perfumed with sea salt. However, Mary hated such situations.

* * *

Shelley and Williams waited for their boat like impatient and spoiled children. Every foreign sail coming from Livorno and skirting the small promontory of Lerici drew them to the beach.

Following Allegra's death, Shelley had written to Captain Roberts asking to change the name of *Don Juan* to *Ariel*. Indeed, everything which could remind him of Byron became horrendous to him. So, he was surprised and angry when the small yacht sailed in with *Don Juan* written in large letters on the sail.

Informed about the request to change the boat's name, Byron became so upset that he ordered Roberts to impose, despite everything, the diabolical seal on the small Platonic boat. With warm water, soap and a brush, Shelley and Williams set to work to clean their poor boat from infamy.

They failed. They used turpentine, without any success. They consulted experts who told them that the only solution was to cut out the name and then sew back the sail. Shelley did not give in, the sail was cut and sewed again.

The Genovese captain who brought the boat said it was good, rapid, and not too difficult to sail, even in bad weather. Williams and Shelley, both incompetent enthusiasts, had requested a copy of a royal yacht, which had a design they admired: to achieve this, two tons of lead had been used to balance it; however, even with this, it remained quite capricious.

The two owners of *Ariel* wanted to sail with just one ship's boy. Williams had sailed for the past three years and pretended to know all about it. Shelley was as clumsy as a woman but had immense willpower. Sometimes, he entangled himself in the riggings, or, used to read Sophocles when at the helm, and often nearly fell overboard. But never had he been so happy. When Trelawny saw him busy in the boat, he took Williams by the arm and advised him to look for a good mariner, someone from the area. "Shelley! You will never do anything good with him unless you cut his hair, throw the tragic Greeks into the sea and put his arms deep in a bucket of tar." Williams was upset. He was a captain himself, and Shelley should be able to help.

Ariel's hull was too deep to land on Casa Magni beach. Williams, with the help of a carpenter, built a tiny rowing boat with tarmacked hessian and a wooden structure for going to and from the *Ariel* to the coast. It was such a fragile vessel, which could capsize easily. However, it became Shelley's favourite thing. He just loved to be rocked along the waves in such a light and tiny basket.

One evening, he saw Jane with her two children on the beach. He invited her to join him in his basket: "with a bit of caution, we can find place for everybody." She huddled in the boat, whose sides sank until only one hand above the water; the slightest wind or one small movement from the children could have made them capsize.

She thought that Shelley just wanted to sail along the shallow banks; however, proud and wanting to show off his rower's skills, he pushed on the oars and soon, they were in the deep blue water of the bay; there, he stopped and fell into a deep reverie. Jane felt overwhelmed with terror and tried quietly to ask a few questions. He did not reply. Then, he lifted his head. He appeared to be animated by a sudden idea, he then said joyfully: "Let's go together and resolve the great mystery!"

If Jane had cried out, her children would have been lost. If Shelley had made a sudden movement, or if the boat had tilted even slightly, the water would have enveloped them. Brightly, she replied: "No, thank you, not now; I would like first to have dinner, and the children wish the same… For that matter, here is Edward coming back with Trelawny;

they will be surprised to find us at sea and Edward would certainly say that this boat is not safe, really."

"Not safe?" said Shelley, quite offended. "I shall sail to Livorno on it; furthermore, I could go anywhere in it."

Jane felt that the Angel of Death was folding its wings. "Have you not yet written the lyrics for the Indian song?" she idly said. "I have; however, I need you to play again the song to me…"

While speaking, he sailed the boat back into the shallow water. As soon as Jane felt she could touch the bottom, she jumped into the water with her children. It was so sudden that Shelley ended up on the sand, enclosed under the dinghy like a crab under its shell. "Jane, are you crazy?" said her husband, fishing out Shelley. "We would have set you back on land if you had waited a moment."

"Not at all, thank you, I have been lucky… What a horrible coffin it would have been. I shall never get in it again. 'Solving the great mystery!' The biggest mystery of all is him… Who can predict what he will do?... I would like so much to leave this place; I am living here in the company of terror itself."

But Shelley's childlike face appeared innocent and radiant. On that beautiful summer's day, it seemed that nothing could ever spoil his joy. In the evening, under the moonlight, he loved sailing *Ariel* with his friends. Mary, sitting at his feet, resting her head on his knees, recalling the same connection ten years before, when they had crossed the English Channel together in stormy weather. How life revealed itself much more subtle and elusive than they could have imagined, how life had betrayed them so much.

Sitting at the back, Jane would sing an Indian serenade while playing the guitar. Shelley would gaze up through the gentle light of the moon, to the fringes of clouds in the quiet June sky. He was not thinking. He felt his mind dissolving within the pure rays of light and the warm scents of the night. His flesh-and-blood body was melting in a delicious ecstasy. It was as if he had become a vapour trail, floating joyfully through space. The scents of the evening, the moon's rays and Jane's voice, all mixed in mysterious harmony, creating a divine and intimate music in his core. Leaving Earth for a world with purer and more fluid forms, he had finally caught up with the beautiful ghosts, the crystalline palaces and the transparent vapours which had once been his only chosen reality. From that moment, he knew for certain that another universe existed, a harsh and inflexible one. Within this parallel and higher space, animated by the gentle and flowing waves of a song and the invisible movement of luminous spheres, women's jealousy, money issues and political conflict finally appeared to him as minimal, and could not affect his overwhelming happiness. He wanted to lose consciousness, overwhelmed by pleasure, and like Faust, declare to the present moment: "O! Stay, you are so beautiful!"

36
ARIEL SET FREE

For a long time, Shelley had wanted to help his friend Hunt to join them in Italy. His creditors and enemies were making his life quite difficult indeed. He was ready to pay for their travel; however, his current revenue was not sufficient to entertain a family with seven children. He raised the issue many times with Byron. In the end, he managed to get from Byron a promise to create with Hunt a liberal journal to be published in Italy, a journal in which Byron's work would be initially published. This unique privilege would guarantee both the success of the journal and Hunt's fortune. It was indeed a very generous offer from Byron, who himself did not get any benefit from this association, on the contrary. However, he did even more; he agreed to leave to the Hunts the ground floor of his palace in Pisa, and Shelley proposed to furnish it himself. So, everything was organised and Hunt's tribe took to the road.

Not without a few difficulties, they finally arrived at Livorno at the end of June 1822. In the harbour, Trelawny was waiting for them on the *Bolivar*. In great style, Shelley and Williams entered the harbour on board of the *Ariel*. Following demonstrations of warmth and joy, the tribe, led by

Shelley, travelled to Pisa, while Williams waited in Livorno for his friend's return to then sail back home together.

Sadly, the first contact between Hunt and Byron ended up unpleasant. Byron perceived Hunt's political ideas as extreme; but he retained a certain protective affection for Hunt as a truthful writer, a good father and husband, in fact a decent fellow. However, he could not stand his wife Marianne; she was vulgar in so many ways. She was one of those egalitarians who thought about inequality all day long. To demonstrate her refusal to consider Byron an aristocrat, she would be so rude to him that no man, even the humblest, would have tolerated her attitude. As for the lovely Guiccioli, Marianne behaved towards her like an English fishwife. Byron remained polite, but very cold.

After twenty-four hours, the poet became exasperated. The seven children were running all over the house and causing a lot of damage: "A kraal of Hottentots, dirtier and more depraved than any yahoos." Lord Byron looked with disgust at this human scum and put his enormous bulldog on guard duty on the stairs, whispering: "Do not let any little cockney come anywhere near us." He was already bored by the idea of the journal.

Shelley, who was due to leave that day, did not want to abandon Hunt before the final arrangements had been made. He calmed down Byron, preached to Marianne, comforted his friend, and delayed his departure day by day until there was a final agreement. His tenacity always won over Byron's haughty languor. He negotiated the title of the newspaper's first publication to be 'The vision of judgment', which would certainly help make it a successful launch. Williams, who was waiting at Livorno, became nervous and impatient. He had never been separated from his wife for so long and was starting to complain. Shelley wrote note after note to explain his successive delays.

The weather was stiflingly hot at the beginning of July; it was *le soleil d'Italie au rire impitoyable* from the late morning till the early hours of the afternoon. The farmers could not work in the fields. Water was scarce, and everywhere, processions of priests, carrying miraculous statues and icons, prayed for rain to come.

On the morning of the eighth, Shelley arrived in Livorno with Trelawny, went to the bank and bought various items for the household. Then, the three friends walked to the harbour. Trelawny was planning to sail the *Bolivar* alongside the *Ariel*. The sky was progressively clouding over, with a light wind in Lerici's direction. Captain Roberts told them that a storm was likely to happen. Williams, who was eager to leave, replied with reassurance that they would be landing in less than seven hours.

At midday, Shelley, Williams and the ship's boy were on board *Ariel;* Trelawny was on board *Bolivar,* organising himself too. The coastguards' boat came alongside to check their papers: "*Barchetta Don Juan*? Captain Percy Shelley? *Va bene.*" Trelawny, who did not have his port-clearance, tried to divert them with some arguments: the officer threatened to send him to quarantine. He proposed to go and get his legal papers; however, Williams was becoming impatient. In any case, they could not waste time, it was already two in the afternoon; there was not much wind, and leaving now would mean arriving during the night.

Ariel left the harbour together with two Italian feluccas. Trelawny, quite upset, docked and asked for his sails to be set up. While waiting, he followed his friends' boat sailing away with a telescope. The Genoese pilot said: "They should have left this morning, much earlier. At three or four… The boat is standing too much inshore; the current may fix her there."

"The land-breeze should soon help her."

"Or soon, she may get too much breeze," the Genoese replied. "This type of sail on a boat with no deck and without a proper mariner on board, this is simply foolish! Look into the distance: those dark lines, the dirty clouds above and this foam above the water. The Devil himself is at work."

From the end of the pier, Captain Roberts was checking the *Ariel* too; once he lost sight of it, he went up the lighthouse and immediately saw the storm coming in towards the small boat, which soon partly shortened its sails. And then the clouds covered it completely.

In the harbour, the air was hot and oppressive; a kind of heavy quietness seemed to solidify the atmosphere. Trelawny, overwhelmed, went down to his cabin and fell asleep. Sometime later, a sound of chains woke him up; the ship's boy had let down another anchor. Everywhere in the harbour, there was the usual agitation before a storm at sea; some were bringing down sails, masts; others tied up ropes, and anchors squeaked. It then became very dark. The sea seemed opaque darkness itself, like a block of lead; gusts of wind rode the sea without any wrinkling, and large drops of rain bounced back from its surface. Fishing boats crossed at high speed and in a confused manner; one could hear whistling noises mixed with orders and shouting. Suddenly, a formidable roll of thunder covered up any human sounds.

A few hours later, when the sky had cleared, Trelawny and Roberts, with their telescopes, checked at length the gulf. No boat could be seen.

* * *

On the other bank of the gulf, the two women waited for news. Mary was worried and now depressed; this very hot summer was now frightening. It was during such weather that her little William had died. She then looked carefully and with concern at the baby in her arms. He was healthy and feeding happily, but as for her, on this terrace, facing the most beautiful view in the world, she could only feel overwhelmed by sadness.

Without any reason, her eyes filled in with tears: "Anyway," she thought, "when he, my Shelley, when he shall come back, I shall be happy, he shall calm me down; and if his son becomes ill, he shall cure him and shall not stop supporting me."

On the following Monday, Jane received a letter from her husband, dated Saturday: Shelley was still in Pisa, "… if he does not come here by Monday, I will leave and sail a felucca to you; expect me on Monday at the latest."

The day they received this letter, the storm had struck. Mary and Jane, seeing the raging sea, could not imagine for one second that *Ariel*, so fragile, could be at sea. On Tuesday, it rained the whole day: a gentle rain, monotonous, on a sea now too calm. On Wednesday, it became windy, and several feluccas landed. The captain of one of them said that *Ariel* had set sail last Monday; however, Jane and Mary could not trust his words. On Thursday, the wind calmed down again, the two women remained waiting on the terrace; every minute, they thought they could see the high sails of the small boat rounding the cap. At midnight, they were both still on the terrace, but now extremely worried, starting to think that their husbands could have been detained in Livorno with a mysterious illness. As the night developed, Jane became so distressed that she decided to charter a boat in the morning. However, the dawn revealed a stormy sea, and the mariners refused categorically to sail. At midday, letters arrived; there was one from Hunt to Shelley. Mary opened it with trembling hands. She read: "Please, write to us as soon as you land, as the weather deteriorated badly following your departure. We are concerned."

The letter fell from Mary's shaking hands. Jane picked it up, read it and said:

"So, it is all over."

"No, my dear Jane, it is not the end; however, I know this waiting is intolerable. Come with me. Let's go to Livorno. We should go there, and quickly we shall know about our destiny."

The road from Lerici to Livorno went through Pisa. The women stopped and went to Lord Byron to ask if by any chance he had some news. They knocked at the door; an Italian domestic replied loudly: "*Chi è?*"; indeed, it was very late. However, she came and opened the door. Byron was in bed, but Countess Guiccioli, smiling brightly, came to meet them. Seeing Mary's terrible pallor, white as marble, she stopped, quite surprised.

"Where is he? *Sapete alcuna cosa di* Shelley?" Mary asked.

Byron, who had followed his mistress, did not know anything other than that Shelley had left Pisa on Sunday for boarding on Monday, and this despite the bad weather.

Refusing to rest, the two women left for Livorno; they arrived at two o'clock in the morning. The coach took them to an inn where they found neither Trelawny nor Captain Roberts. They went to bed fully dressed and waited there until the next day. At six in the morning, they ran, visiting all the other inns in Livorno. At the Globe Inn they found Roberts, who came downstairs, very shaken and distressed. They were told about what had happened during that terrible week.

However, there was still hope. *Ariel* could have been pushed toward Corsica or Elba with the storm. They sent a courier to go around the gulf to ask if any sign of wreckage had been found. At nine in the morning, they both left to go back to Casa Magni. Trelawny went with them. In crossing Viareggio, they were told that a small boat and a barrel had been found on the beach. Trelawny went to see. It was *Ariel*'s tiny rowing boat. However, there was still the possibility that the rowing boat, cumbersome in stormy weather, might have been thrown overboard on purpose. When Jane and Marry arrived at Casa Magni, the village fair was on. All night long, the loud songs and dancing prevented them from getting any sleep.

* * *

Five to six days later, Trelawny, who had promised a reward to any coastguards with some kind of information, finally got called to Viareggio, where it was said that a corpse had been found on the beach. It was a cadaver, quite gruesome to behold. All the body parts not protected by clothing had been completely shredded by fish. However, the tall and fragile silhouette was so familiar to Trelawny that he could not have the slightest doubt about it. In one of the vest's pockets, he found Sophocles; in the other, a volume of Keats, still open, as if the reader, interrupted by the storm, had put it away quickly. At the same time, the corpses of both Williams and the mariner were given up by the sea, a short distance away, and even more mutilated. Trelawny asked for the bodies to be buried in the sand on the spot to prevent the waves taking them back. Then, in haste, he left for Casa Magni.

At the doorstep, he stopped. Nobody was to be seen; only one light was burning. Maybe the two widows were still retaining some kind of hope. Trelawny remembered his past visits, when the two families had gathered on the terrace, just above the water, calm, and reflecting the stars. He remembered Williams shouting *"Bueno notte!"* when he crossed the bay and rowed to reach the *Bolivar,* while from afar, Jane could be heard singing and playing her guitar. Then, Shelley's ear-splitting voice would make the tranquil air tremble. He remembered so well listening at length and with joy to this once happy family.

His reveries were stopped by a single shout. Caterina, the nanny, walking down the corridor, saw him near the entrance. And so, he went upstairs, and without being announced, entered the bedroom where Mary and Jane were. He did not say anything. Mary's big hazelnut eyes stared at him with such intensity. She exclaimed: "Is there no hope anymore?"

Trelawny, without a word, left the bedroom and asked the nanny to take the children and the two mothers away.

37
THE LAST LINKS

Mary had wanted Shelley to be buried with his son, in the cemetery in Rome that he had found so beautiful. However, this was not permitted by Italian sanitary laws. A corpse washed ashore could not be buried let alone transported. Trelawny suggested that his two friends should be cremated and proposed to set up a pyre on the beach in the fashion of Ancient Greece. When the day for the ceremony was fixed, he asked for Byron and Hunt to be informed. Trelawny decided to sail to the funeral in the *Bolivar*. The Tuscan authorities appointed a squad of soldiers, clothed for the task and equipped with shovels and pickaxes.

Williams's corpse was the first to be exhumed from the sandy soil. Standing around, his friends observed in silence the work of the soldiers and awaited the first human remains with a mix of sadness, horror and curiosity. A corner of a black handkerchief appeared first, then a collar, and then the body itself, in such a decomposed state that, when the soldiers touched them, the limbs detached themselves from the torso. Then, the soldiers started to work at it with large pincers resembling torture tools.

Byron stared at the misshapen heap of flesh and bones and said: "So, this is a human body? It looks rather like a sheep's carcass."

He was terribly emotional, his forced, detached demeanour was a way to hide his feelings, which he considered plebeian. When the soldiers were about to collect the skull, he added: "I can recognise any man I have spoken to by looking at his teeth… I always observe the mouth, as it says what the eyes try to hide."

A high pyre made of pine wood had been built. Trelawny approached it with a torch. A great resinous flame went up in the still atmosphere. The heat became so fierce that the spectators had to move back. The bones, when burning, gave the flame a silver sparkle of exquisite purity; when the fire died down a little, Byron and Hunt went closer and threw incense on the funeral bed, together with salt and wine. "Let's go," Byron said, "let's go and try the violent sea which has drowned our friends… How many knots away from the shore were they at the time they capsized, do we know?"

It is probable that at that very moment, sadness was mingling with his own conviction that he, Lord Byron who swam the Hellespont, would not have been submerged by this sea with such small waves. He took off his clothes, jumped in the water and quickly swam away.

Trelawny and Hunt followed suit. From afar, the pyre became a small sparkling stain on the beach.

* * *

The next day, it was Shelley's turn. His body had been buried in the sand closer to Viareggio, between the sea and the pine forest.

The weather was beautiful. Under strong sunlight, the vivid yellow sand and the purple sea created a startling contrast. Above the trees, the white summits of the Apennine mountains seemed part of a cloudy, marble-like background, which Shelley himself had admired so much.

A number of children came from the village to see this rare spectacle; however, a respectful silence was observed. Even Byron was quiet, thoughtful and sad: "O, Iron man," he thought, "that is now what is left from such courage… You wanted to defy Jupiter, Prometheus… And here you are…"

The soldiers continued digging without finding any sign of the corpse, when suddenly, a hard and empty noise alerted everyone that one of the pickaxes had hit the skull. Byron shivered. He suddenly thought of Shelley: once, with him on the lake at Geneva on a stormy day; his arms crossed, in a posture together heroic and hopeless, which appeared to him a perfect symbol for this beautiful man: "How wrong people who judged him have been… He has been the best, the least selfish man I have ever known… And what a gentleman he used to be! The most perfect one who had ever entered a club!"

The soldiers covered up the body in lime. Incense, oil and salt were scattered in the fire, and the wine flowed like water. The heat made the air shimmer. After three hours, Shelley's heart, which was surprisingly enlarged, had still not been consumed by the flames: Trelawny plunged his hand into the fire and took the relic. The skull, which had been broken in two by a soldier's pickaxe, opened and revealed the brain boiling away, as if in a cauldron.

Byron could not stand it anymore. Like the night before, he jumped completely naked into the water and swam to the *Bolivar*, anchored in the bay. Trelawny collected Shelley's ashes and whitened bones in a funerary urn he had brought with him. It was made of oak and lined with black velvet. The local children, watching him with intense curiosity, told each other that if the ashes were brought back to England, the dead will be reborn again.

* * *

Maybe, we should explain what next happened to the principal characters of this story.

Sir Timothy Shelley lived until the age of ninety-one. Mary received a small pension from him, but she had to promise not to publish any posthumous poems or even the biography of her husband while the baronet was still alive. When he died, Percy-Florence inherited the title and wealth, since Harriet's son had died in early infancy.

The tragedy united the two widows, Mary and Jane. They lived together for quite a while, in Italy and then in London. The friends of her respective husbands were so faithful that Trelawny ended up proposing to Mary, and later, Hogg, the sceptic, proposed to Jane. Mary refused, with the argument that she quite liked the name Mary Shelley, a name so beautiful, she would never be able to depart from it. Jane accepted; however, on the day of the wedding she declared that she had never been married to Williams and that she had a husband somewhere in India. Hogg did not care about it and they lived together without bothering about marriage; they never left each other, and led a decent life. Despite being precise and hardworking, Hogg was considered a rather average lawyer; he lacked eloquence and warmth. By the end of his life, he had become a shy, old, disillusioned man, who limited his reading to Greek and Latin in a humble attempt to avoid boredom.

Claire stayed on the continent and became a teacher in Russia. When Sir Timothy died, she was finally able to get out of her misery with a significant sum of money, which Shelley had bequeathed to her.

The older they grew, the more quarrelsome the three women became. Jane claimed that Shelley had been in love with her during the last months in Pisa and Casa Magni. Her words were reported to Mary who, very upset, decided never to see her again. Then, Jane transformed herself slowly but surely into a slightly deaf old woman, kind, whose eyes sparkled when she spoke of the poet.

Claire worked for a few years on a book; she had wanted to demonstrate the necessity of considering love as trivial to be happy, taking Shelley and Byron as examples. However, she lost her mind and had to take a long rest. She finished her life in Florence, where she converted to Catholicism and worked with charitable institutions.

Around 1879, a young man who was working on some documentation about Byron and Shelley visited Claire. As soon as he pronounced the two names, behind the old woman's wrinkles, he saw the young woman's smile, which had made her so charming at twenty: a smile rather shy, yet still full of hope and promise. "And so," she said, "I suppose that you are thinking like the others: you think that I was in love with Byron, don't you?"

She continued, as he gazed at her with astonishment: "My young friend," she said, "one day will come when you shall better understand a woman's heart. I was amazed by Byron; however, I was not in love… I could have been… however, it did not happen."

A long silence settled, then the investigator, with some hesitation, finally asked:

"Lady, have you ever been in love?"

She blushed and, without answering, she looked down at the floor.

"Shelley?" he murmured, with a nearly imperceptible voice.

"With all my heart and with all my soul," said the old woman passionately, without raising her eyes.

Then, with a charming flirtatious gesture, she gave the young man a tap on his cheek.

Love Your Book

Ariel Percy Bysshe Shelley

TIMELINE

JANUARY 2025

Soft-back book printed from paper that has been carbon offset through the World Land Trust Scheme.

PRINTED by Hobbs the Printers Ltd
at Southampton, United Kingdom

PUBLISHED by Cybirdy Publishing
London, United Kingdom

SPECIAL EDITION

Ariel Percy Bysshe Shelley

WHO are you?	WHO did you obtain the book from?	WHEN did you obtain the book
FIRST GUARDIAN		
SECOND GUARDIAN		
THIRD GUARDIAN		
FOURTH GUARDIAN		
FIFTH GUARDIAN		